Romance on the Hector

Do enjoy —

Marianne White

Marianne Guimond White

Published by Lydwin Publishing, June 2023
ISBN: 9781739042608

Typeset: Red Tuque Books
Book Cover Design: Red Tuque Books

Acknowledgements

For Gary who opened so many doors to the world around me. Always, encouraging and inspiring me to follow my lifes dreams. When times were bleak, you inspired me to forge on towards another opportunity that was waiting just around the next corner. Forever supportive and confident in my fixation, to persue and grow creatively.

My son Neal and daughter Anne Marie, who are shadows of their father in so many ways, that it comforts me. You both have unique ways of expressing possitive vibes, towards any venture or path I have chosen to move towards. You are the blessing that I thank for every day as the sun sets.

My writers' group, *"Pictou County Writers - New and Experienced."* Located in New Glasgow, NS. An inspirating group that always assured me that I was a storyteller and author. Turning my self-doubt and apprehension towards assurance and appreciation regarding my creative poems and short stories. Providing me with the confidence to say those beautiful words. *"I am a Writer and Author."*

Huge gratitude to Greg Salisbury, owner of Red Tuque Books Inc. An exceptionally talented and patient editor, with a sharp editorial eyes for detail. Without his guidance and support, this novella would not have been published.

Dedication

This historical prose full of romance and mystery would never have been written had it not been for the ancestors and descendants of the first Scottish settlers who took a chance for a better way of life. Travelling aboard the historic vessel built in the Netherlands and was christened *"Hector."*

On that misty morn, July 15th, 1773, sailing across the vast ocean waters. Towards unkown shores to a place that earlier settlers had christened New Scotland, locate in a virgin country of Canada. (New Scotland is now known a Nova Scotia.)

Chapter 1

Loch Broom, Scotland

A hush came over the room, as I suddenly pushed the large oak wooden door open. My vision focused on the shadowy silhouette of four adults sitting around our family's dinner table.

I stood hovering over the threshold, of our small Scottish dwelling. The darkened confinement of the room enveloped me. Advancing further into the dimly lit space, my vision gradually grew clearer. Now having a better view of the four adults who sat around the table. Surprised to see such a distinguished couple gathered with my parents conversing.

All eyes turned to focus on me as I stepped into the large residence and closed the door. Suddenly, extremely confident that this instant silence was all about me.

Who was this distinguished-looking couple? Not a local sheep herder, like my family and our surrounding neighbours.

Not recalling a time when my family's home had the pleasure of such rich and uniquely dressed travellers.

The velvety wine-coloured, riding habit this female guest wore was professionally tailored by an extremely talented professional. Most definitely of Georgian design. Her embroidered garment, a double-breasted bodice, with a stand-up three-inch collar, was stylish.

Studying this beautiful, unique lady I was confident she was wearing a lace stay corset beneath her riding jacket. This garment provides an hourglass-alluring figure that an elegant lady loved to portray. Directing a male's vision to focus on a woman's alluring slim waistline enhances her bosom.

This striking woman's chestnut brown hair was styled in perfect soft waves. At the back of her neck, small, twisted curls were arranged to fall between her neck and the high collar of her jacket. These ringlet bouncy curls fell over her front bodice ending a few inches from the lace that covered her bosom. She sat on the bench that was always used for the children of our family. My mother sat beside her instead of her own chair at the end of the table.

The unique handsome gentleman then occupied my attention. He sat cross-legged in my mother's chair at the end of the trestle table. He wore a full-skirted knee-length coat. With matching knee breeches, and long white silk stockings. He wore stacked black pointed leather shoes with a detachable silver buckle on his feet.

My father sat in his usual spot at the head of the table. He was the first to speak, saying; *"Maddie come sit by me, we have an important discussion we need to share with you."*

My family had been calling me this nickname since I

was a wee lass. The name they christened me was Madeline.

An obedient daughter I stepped further into the room and headed to the bench behind the long table. Sitting at my designated spot for all our family meals. My mother sat next to me. The elegantly dressed lady sat on the other side of my mother, close to her husband.

My father spoke slowly, *"This is Laird Donald and Lady Fraser from the county of Cromartyshire. They have a proposition for our family."* Continuing he says, *"Your mother and I have discussed it and agreed with this offer from Laird and Lady Fraser. It is the best for our family and your future. Coming to the decision was exceedingly difficult for your mother and me to come to."*

Looking from him to my mother, then to the two unexpected guests at the end of the table. Puzzled as to what my father was talking about.

Lady Fraser spoke first, *"Maybe it's best if I was the one to explain."* Continued saying, *"My husband and I are in need of a Governess to look after our three children."* She pauses, placing her hand over the small bump protruding from her abdomen. Raising her vision, looking straight at me and continues. *"And soon to have one more in the next few months making it four children all under the age of ten. A task too grand for myself and my husband."* Pausing she turns her vision and now focuses on her husband. This elegant lady raises her hand from her lap and placed it over her husband's that rested on our wooden table. Giving his hand a gentle squeeze.

Laird Fraser turns his vision away from his wife. His focus is on my dark brown eyes saying, *"My wife and I need a governess to help care for our children. We were hoping you would accept our offer to join our family. If you decide to accept this position, you will live with us in our home and have your own room. You will travel with us wherever we go. You will be treated as family. Your*

3

only responsibility is to watch over our children, teach them, be their personal Tudor in their studies, and play and entertain them. Is this something you wish to do?"

I sat overwhelmed by this offer. Being the oldest and always watching over my siblings, reading to them, and teaching them the appropriate studies for their ages. To do it for a stranger's family, in their home was making my head spin.

Could I leave my home and family? I wondered.

Was I ready for this challenge?

My mother's hand reaches under the table grabbing hold of my small fingers and giving them a slight squeeze. Sending endorsing signals thru my fingers into my small frame. Assuring me that I was able to take on this task.

However, wondering was I ready to leave my family. I turn to look into my father's eyes and recall his comment as I entered the room. They were aware of this offer and had previously discussed it with this striking couple.

Remembering his words. *"Your mother and I have discussed .... It's the best for your future."*

"The best for MY future." I thought as I recalled his words.

It's my future they were thinking about. They were looking out for my well-being.

Wanting what was best for me. Even thou they may never see me again.

It was me they were thinking about. Concerned about me.

Yes, Me, the eldest daughter of William Ross.

Arriving at our home, inquiring if they could hire me as their Governess for their three young children. Sarah just turned six, Matthew was age four, and Samuel was only eighteen months old. Mistress Fraser was pregnant with her fourth child.

Everyone was aware the duration of this ocean voyage could possibly last a few weeks. Laird and Lady Fraser required help managing to keep their young children entertained during this arduous journey. Lord Fraser was aware they may be confined in the bowels of this tall sailing ship for days. Traversing across the vast blue ocean waters could take several weeks, possibly more.

Perplexed by this request to be childcare worker for their children. I have mixed feelings. Saddened because I would have to leave my family for an unknown country. Not knowing if I will ever see them or my young siblings again.

However, excited at the same time for this overwhelming opportunity regarding this expedition to travel to this new world our Scottish neighbours often spoke of.

Chapter 2

My father had been struggling to feed our family of five children all under the age of seventeen. I'm the oldest of the Ross children and will be turning eighteen after the passing of two crescent moons, recalling how my father taught me the task of a shearer, removing the wool coat from our herd of sheep. It was my mother who patiently taught me how to card the sheared wool, spinning and weaving it into stands for knitting garments. Recalling how she sat patiently showing me how to knit, sew and cook. At a young age, my father taught me how to read, and manage the accounts for our family sheep farm. Other local sheep farmers soon requested I help them maintain their ledgers for their sheep herds.

Last week when, my parents, met with that distinguished couple. Lord Fraser, a brother to Laird John Fraser of the parish of Kintail. An estate where my family would be leaving to start a new beginning.

Lord Donald Fraser and his family were on the list of passengers, seeking passage aboard the Ship Hector, which was leaving Loch Broom in the Scottish Highlands. Heading for a new life in the Birthplace of New Scotland located in the large new country called "CANADA."

A gentleman by the name of Master John Ross was hired as a recruiter by Mr. Pagan along with Mr. Witherspoon. Owners of Ship Hector to find families willing to move to the New World across the vast ocean.

Arriving here to offer these families free passage, one year's free provisions, and productive farmland, across the vast water to a new settlement.

Nearly Two Hundred Scottish settlers signed to board the ship Hector on the second week of July in the year 1773. The list confirmed approximately 188 passengers were to travel, stating, there were Twenty- Five (25) single men. As well as twenty-three (23) families and children. Thirty (30) of the children were under two years of age.

These Scottish families were all excited and looking forward to a fresh start, a new beginning. In another strange country, they would eventually call the birthplace of New Scotland. Situated along the eastern coast of a vast large open country called CANADA.

Hearing so much about these new lands every time the tinker man travelled through our small village. He repeated stories he obtained from the sailors as they disembarked, onto the large wooden wharf in Loch Broom.

During the brutal battle of Culloden, also known as the Highland Clearance. A word I was so familiar with because this was my family. This is where I was raised, and the only way of life I was familiar with.

I heard many stories about the Battle of Culloden including the implementation of the "Dress Act of 1746." This historic battle had left my parents and their families homeless and destitute These handed-down tales passed on by my parents and relatives were retold so many times. After the devastation between the Jacobites and the English army, how it tore families apart? Scattering them to various parts of Scotland. Away from their historical homes and family residents.

Many Scottish Villages were targeted following this historic Battle. English resentment over the Jacobite rebellion festered over so many years. The whole country was essentially under martial law and the British army could do what it wished. There were many atrocities, whole communities were burned to the ground.

The British Parliament also set forth the "Draconian Act", discarding the Highlands' dress in Public. Proclaiming it a serious offence for the Highlanders to dress in their family colours. Barring them from wearing their Tartan, Kilts, or Plaids.

They had to wear the clothing of the Sassenach (a lowlander). Also, a serious offence for Highlanders to possess Fire Arm. These Scottish northerners were given one year to purchase trousers or sew them, themselves.

"Draconian Act; The Dress Act of 1746.
Abolition and Proscription of the Highland Dress: From and after the first day of August,
One thousand, seven hundred and forty-seven,
no man or boy within that part of Britain called Scotland, other than such as shall be employed as
Officers and Soldiers in His Majesty's Forces,

shall, on any pretext whatever,
wear or put on the clothes commonly called Highland
clothes, the Plaid, (that is to say) the Plaid Philabeg,
or little Kilt, Trowse, Shoulder belts,
or any part what ever of what
peculiarly belongs to the Highland Garb...
For the first offence,
shall be liable to be imprisoned for 6 months,
and on the second offence,
to be transported to any of
His Majesty's plantations beyond the seas."

After this devastating war, these Scottish Gaelic Highlanders were divided into three separate categories; One-Third of them were called "Whigs a supporter of British Policies.

Another third; was "Neutral." The last group remaining, were the Jacobites, supporters of the young Prince Charles Edward, Duke of Edinburgh Scotland.

Many Scottish towns and villages were targeted following this historical battle of Culloden as English resentment over the Jacobite rebellion festered over the following years.

The only regions of Scotland that had little or no effect from this historic rebellion were the Scottish Highlands. These northern mountain regions were too rugged with impossible terrain.

Traversing these jagged rocky regions was almost unmanageable. Trails were nothing more than cow paths. Most of the rugged terrain where hopeless for animals due to the rocky mountainous territory. Unable to traverse by foot soldiers.

Areas that were unable to harvest oats or barley, due to eroding slopes. Neglected by the government and cut off for most of the year by severe weather conditions. These Scottish nomad settlers were known as Wild Highlanders.

Chapter 3

Many families were forcibly removed from their Ancestral homes. Hearing there was a better option across the Ocean. Word of a New Scotland was spreading throughout the highland. Stories from the returning tall ships that had successfully transported many of their clan members to this new land. Being told they could find a better way of life on the other side of these vast blue waters to a land called North America.

Whenever these tall sailing ships came into the harbour. The travelling tinkers were there to purchase new bolts of fabric, cooking utensils, farm tools, and stylish clothing arriving from other ports of call from around the world. They told stories and tales that were shared by weary sailors on their return home.

Gathered in the local Inns, regaling over a pint of beer, ale, and sometimes a mug full of wine that was smuggled aboard ship from Italy, Spain, and France.

These sailors were ready with an abundance of stories of their sailing journeys to the many towns and ports they stopped along their dangerous, however exciting voyages at sea.

As an avid reader, I absorbed these words printed on the pages of a book like a sponge. Wanting to witness these beautiful experiences as well. That intrigued and captivated me. My imagination took me to a part of the world I could only dream of. Hoping deep down that someday I would be visiting them for myself.

This unique and interesting position I have just been offered was going to fulfil many of my desires and wishes that I had read and dreamt about.

Several days later I became aware that there was more to my acceptance of this Governess position. The conversation these four adults had prior to my entrance held another offer.

If I accepted to join the Fraser family as Governess and travel with them on this trans-Atlantic excursion. In turn, my father would be provided with a position with housing at the Manor located in the parish of Kintail, one-half mile from Evanton Ville. My father would be responsible for all the Sheep Herders working on the Lord John Fraser Estate. A fair size cottage located on the estate would be home for my parents and siblings.

My family was parting, and going in different directions, however, moving towards positive opportunities for a better future.

Today is a very dark miserable day. As I rose from my bed I shared with my young siblings. Leaving our small thatch home was most heart-breaking. This place has been my childhood home since my birth. A home filled with over seventeen years of wonderful memories.

How was I going to be able to leave all this? I wonder as I pack my few possessions.

Concerned, about how my parents must feel about me leaving. Heartbroken, I am sure.

I turn, watching them as they packed the items in our small kitchen.

Pondering! Are they anxious and happy about this separation of their family or are they sad? So many cherished memories our family shared in this small dwelling.

Standing in the doorway, holding the few belonging that was my only possessions, I turn sadly embracing each of my siblings. My parents were the last to take me into their comforting arms. Knowing this may be the last time we ever embrace. My family was packing our belongings in a small Scottish market town in the highlands. Preparing to leave for the parish of Kintail.

Sad feelings as I leave my family cottage on the outskirts of the small district of Braes of Ullapool on the eastern shores of the "LOCH." Working my way down the hillside. That had been my home since my birth.

Descending towards the slow-moving river. Through the clearing, my vision catches the calm crystal waters of the Loch.

Standing, looking over the horizon, frozen, reflecting on the meaning of this Scottish word, *"a lake or an arm of water coming in from the sea as it narrows into the land. Flowing and blending with the small rivers and streams falling from the top of these Scottish Highlands."*

As I pause to view this beautiful overwhelming vision. I may never see it again. Needing to burn it into my memory, never wishing to forget the place of my birth.

A slight shiver envelops my body as I step into the clearing. The weather becomes a bit cooler as I meander closer to the open bay. Today is a cool brisk and invigorating morn for an early July day. Pulling my knitted wool shawl tighter around my upper chest.

Gripping my homemade carpet satchel, a little tighter. It is filled with additional garments and my toiletry provisions. Swung on my back I carry a woven sack filled with chalk and a few slate slabs for teaching. Along with an ample collection of novels that were donated by many friends and families. All necessary items for the young children in my care.

In the distance, my vision focuses on the three masts of the tall ship that would take me to this new county called Canada that the locals have been talking about.

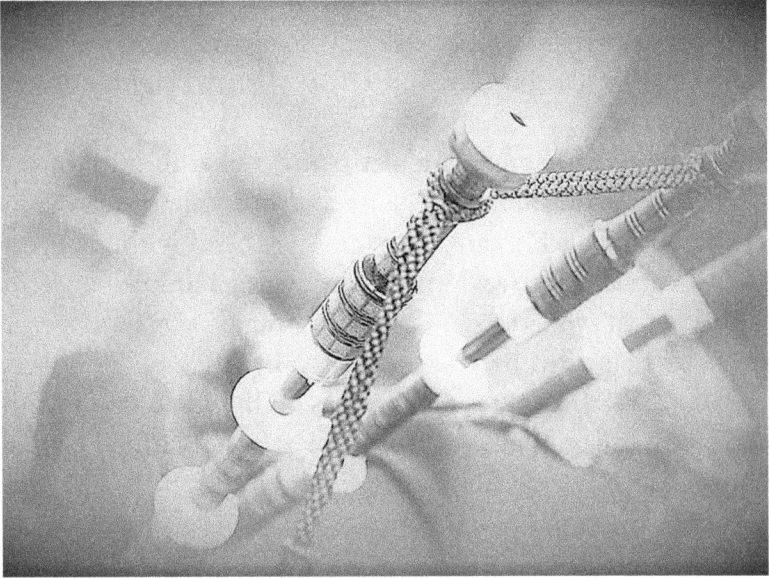

Chapter 4

Arriving closer to the Harbour, I finally reach the old wooden wharf that stretches along the calm bay of Loch Broom. Approaching closer my vision focuses on the large vessel anchored in the harbour. Before me, a beautiful tall sailing ship sitting so majestic gleaming in the sunshine. Near the bow of the ship, on one of the wide black planks the word, "HECTOR" in large brass letters shines in the sunlight. This was the ship that was going to take me on an unknown adventure. Across the vast ocean waters to another county that the locals have been calling New Scotland.

I stop frozen, wanting to absorb this view. Capturing it into my memory for a lifetime.

My small frame is suddenly overwhelmed with mixed

emotions. Saddened, never to witness it ever again as I board this large vessel. And sail away to New Scotland situated across these vast blue waters.

Strolling along the long wooden dock. I walk over to a stack of wooden crates that were sitting on the weathered wharf boards.

I notice a crew of young men placing large wooden grates onto a woven rope net. Rising it into the air by a swinging pulley. Lowering its heavy load over the side of the wharf onto a barge below. My vision catches movement in the water alongside the ship. A crew of two was using large poles to push a floating empty raft back towards the wharf. The two floating rafts pass along each other the men shouting laughing comments to their passing mates.

My body was in desperate need of rest from the long journey. Leaving my family home on the other side of the bay. Resting my back against another crate looking out at the massive, huge ocean vessel bobbing as the current rises in the bay.

My main field of vision watching as the dock workers hoisted large nets, holding crates loaded with supplies for our long ocean voyage.

A ruckus draws my attention to my left. Beside me stands a young gentleman wearing a white neck-tied tunic tucked into a well-worn pair of black britches secured with a small rope. At his feet sat a partially opened tattered canvas sack, my eye caught sight of his blue and green Highland Plaid and sporran. His bagpipes hung on his hip, his arms moving to create the sounds of an olde Scottish ballad.

Was he here to greet the departing passengers? I look at him in wonder-meant, as I sat so exhausted and weary from my long journey.

When he completed his ballad, I turned to him saying; *"that was beautiful, what's your name?"*

"William MacKay, lass, what is your clan's name?"

"Ross, I am the daughter of William Ross from Cromarty, located, in the Highlands. My name is Madeline, but everyone calls me Maddie."

"Are you here to board the ship to New Scotland?" He inquires as he pointed to the large vessel.

"Yes, I am travelling with Lord and Lady Fraser from the Ross-Shire, also from Northern Highlands. What about you, are you also travelling on this ship, to this New World?"

"I'm hoping to, however, I can't come up with the fare they are asking for."

Directing my vision to his black well worn, polished shoes. His shoe touches the tin cup that sat on one of the deck boards in front of him. *"My vessel has only a few shillings, not enough to cover my passage."*

"OH! I'm sorry, to hear that."

"I still have hope, there is plenty of time before the ship sails." He pauses for a moment, then said; *"I'll continue to stand here and play until she leaves the bay."*

"Aren't you afraid the British will seize your bagpipes or your Highland Plaids in your sack?"

He looked down at his open sack giving it a slight kick, hiding his Plaid, and says, *"I'll take my chances."*

Turning adjusting my seating position on the stack of crates, I reply, *"Good luck collecting enough funds for your fair. I will pray they don't come and catch you before the ship departs."*

Removing the tied sack that was slung over my shoulder. Gently placing it down by my feet, on a wide board-walk plank. Manoeuvring my small frame on the crate, resting my aching back against the cool wood of the large box. Closing my eyes, I listen to the familiar Scottish tunes the man next to me was playing. The heat of the mid-afternoon sun warms my small frame.

Relaxing, feeling rested, my vision now turns to a young male dock worker, in the opposite direction. Watching this young lad at work, I began to wonder, was he a dock worker or possibly a crew member for the large ship? Sitting, contemplating my wandering thoughts, when the answer to my question was revealed before my eyes.

Chapter 5

This tall young sailor was removing his slope. (A loose garment also known as a shipmen's smock.)

Watching in shock, as he lowers the suspenders of his breeches. Then pulls the tails of the crisp white smock from his loose pantaloons. Crossing his arms, he reached for the bottom of his smock rising it up and over his head. Exposing his bare muscular chest. He then took the garment and wiped the droplet of sweat falling from his forehead that had been seeping into his vision. Lowering the bunched garment from his face, his eyes connected with mine.

Ashamed that I was caught staring at him. I quickly move my head to the left, my vision now focused on the large brass letters of the ship's name. Embarrassed, that at my young age I was watching a man undress, exposing his naked frame.

He approaches, coming closer to where I sat on the stack of crates. Standing beside me his tall frame created a darkened shadow, blocking the warmth of the sun that had been embracing my slender body.

My vision slowly moves to the most beautiful blue eyes I had ever seen. A frosty blue, like the sea on a calm Scottish winter day. However, revealing a slight twinkle that could be very mischievous.

With a teasing smile, he throws his garment. It falls on a crate, next to the one I was resting on. My eyesight quickly lowers in embarrassment. He remains standing before me, my vision level with the double row of buttons holding the flap on the front of his dark blue knee-length trousers. Exposing his flat bare abdomen with darkened ripples around his naval.

Startled and extremely embarrassed that I was seeing a man who bared his body in such a manner in the presents of a woman.

Quickly jumping from the crate, and standing I inquire, *"Do I need to move?"*

"No lass, those crates will be the last ones to get loaded on the ship." was his reply.

Continuing he states, *"Your welcome to stay right there, I'll let you know when you need to move."*

All I could do was nod my head and lower my vision, feeling so uncomfortable. Embarrassed as I looked at his bare chest. My father was the only man I had ever seen bare-chested. This tanned man's barely clad body had a small collection of dark black chest hairs. Visible between his breast nipples.

So shy, and feeling uncomfortable, I lowered my body back to sit on the crate. My vision quickened to downcast and focused on the darkened wharf boards at my feet. Unable to view his facial features up close. My demeanour was thrown into a tizzy, I sat frozen on the crate. Not sure where I should direct my field of vision. Confident that if I tried to look up towards his face, I would not be able to move them beyond his bare chest.

Still standing before me. The shadow of his body blocked the ray of sun that was previously providing heat over my cool slender frame.

He inquires: *"Are you a passenger on the Hector?"*

Timidly, I raised my eyesight to view the ship as it slightly swayed in the harbour, I then scanned the sky, slowly moving my vision towards his face. Assuring myself that if I kept my vision above his chin I could reply to his questions without embarrassment.

Looking into those deep-sea blue eyes I say, *"Yes I'm travelling by ship, with Lord and Lady Fraser and their family."*

He inquires; *"Why are you travelling with Lord and Lady Fraser and his family instead of your own family?"*

"My family is remaining in Scotland; I have been hired as the Governess for the children of the Fraser family. I was directed to meet then at the wharf before the ship's departures," I replied.

"A governess you say, what does a governess do?" he inquires.

"My responsibility is to care for their young children, teaching them to read and write. Keeping them entertained."

"So, you are a teacher then?" was his response.

"Well, yes, I guess I am." pausing to look towards the blue sky, removing my vision from those intriguing alluring hypnotic eyes of his.

Taking a deep breath, I lower my site and continued *"I will be teaching them as well as looking after them. Lady Fraser is with child and is unable to care for them during her pregnancy."*

"Are you staying with them over the next few days?" He inquires.

Shocked by his question, I quickly returned my focus to his face and spoke. *"No, why?"*

"It will take us at the very least, a few more days to load all of these crates and cartons onto the ship," pausing he continues, *"Where are you staying?"*

I became startled by his comment.

Recalling, Lord Fraser's words to me when he departed our family home. *"Meet us at the wharf when the ship arrives in port and is ready to depart."*

Unaware that it would take time to unload the ship from its journey. Then having to reload the vessel with new supplies for our long voyage across the Atlantic.

Startled at the disturbing revelation, my sudden reaction of shock and sadness as I instantly became aware of this troubling miss understanding. I lowered my head into my hands and quietly cried. Shocked by my unfortunate demise.

Chapter 6

The young deckhand knelt before me, gently placing his hand on my left elbow, saying. *"Why are you weeping?"*

I pulled an embroidered cotton handkerchief from my bosom and dabbed away the tears that fell down my cheek. Recalling Lord Fraser's words, I repeated them out loud, saying; *"Lord Fraser told me I should be at the wharf shortly after the ship arrives in port."* I raise my head and look into those memorable blue eyes of this young lad.

Continued in whimpering sobs; *"At no time did the Frasers inform me there would be a delay of several days. I have no place to go. I can't go back home, my parents have already left for their new position at the castle, located in Cromartyshire in the Northern Highlands. It is owned by the Clan Fraser; my father has taken a position as a Serf for Lord Fraser's' brother. What am I to do? Where can I stay? My family has already departed on their long journey."*

Lowering my head into my hands and let the tears fall uncontrollably. It was not long before my small nappy was sopping wet, and no longer served its purpose.

The young lad reaches for his discarded tunic that he had thrown on the crate earlier. Gently bring it to my face, wiping the flood of tears that flowed from my moist sad eyes.

With each gentle wipe of his cotton garment, he softly assures me that all would be fine. He would find a way to help me with my troublesome dilemma. With his tall muscular frame squatted before me, my vision remained on those beautiful hypnotic blue eyes.

The masculine scent from his garment was comforting and somehow alluring. I noticed a heavy musky scent of heather and floral making the damp garment smell like a summer breeze. I gently wiped the salty moist tears from my face, then passed the soaked shirt back to the young man.

As he reached for his drenched shirt he said, *"My name is Malcolm Lyon, everyone calls me Mackie."*

With a low mumble, *"My name is Madeline Ross, and everyone calls me Maddie."* Lowering my head, I continued in a whisper. *"I'm sorry I soaked your shirt,"* I reply with a mortified soft voice.

"No problem. It is unfortunate that Lord Fraser was not very clear with you regarding the departure time of the sailing vessel."

"I don't know what I'm going to do."

"Not to worry, the captain won't be returning until all the crates, boxes, and bags are loaded on the ship and stored in the hole." Mackie turns to extend his arms to show the large

quantity of stacked cartons and boxes placed along the wharf.

Continuing he says, *"Looking at the many piles my guess is, it's going to take several days before we get it completed."*

Shocked by his comment, I reply, *"So where am I going to stay and eat if it takes several days?"*

"I must get back to work. Please do not leave. I will make sure you get a place to spend your nights and ensure you get something to eat. So, please stay right here."

Remaining seated on the crate. I open my sack and remove one of my novels. Choosing a book of sonnets written by the historic author and play-write William Shakespeare. Of the One Hundred and Fifty-Four (154) written Sonnets, in the small novel.

My choice was the second (second) Sonnet.

> *"When Forty Winters Shall Besiege Thy Brow."*
> *And dig deep trenches in thy beauty's field,*
> *Thy youth's proud livery so gazed on now,*
> *Will be a tattered weed, of small worth held.*
> *Then being asked where all thy beauty lies—*
> *Where all the treasure of thy lusty days—*
> *To say within thine own deep-sunken eyes*
> *Were an all-eating shame and thriftless praise.*
> *How much more praise deserved thy beauty's use.*
> *If thou couldst answer "This fair child of mine*
> *Shall sum my count and make my old excuse."*
> *Proving his beauty by succession thine.*
> *This was to be new made when thou art old,*
> *And see thy blood warm when thou feel'st it cold."*

After reading these fourteen lines of The Shakespearean Sonnet, I sat back placing the hard-cover book on my lap and reflected on these beautiful words. Resting my head against the large wooden crate, I closed my eyes. Recalling these touching phrases, thoughts of my mother come flooding into my mind.

"How forty winters have touched her beautiful skin.
Where exposed creases and deepened, facial features reside.
Her eyes now darkened with worries,
and sunken with concerns for each of her children.
Where has her smooth younger face gone?
Passed on at the birth to each of her children.
Created by the love connection between two eternal lovers.
Love creates a bond, a fire of emotions, and blends together,
resulting in a bairn.
Her proud motherly stature expects the arrival of each new life.
She will carry and share these memorable accounts,
of her life's journey while on this earth.
Assured she has not made any misuse of her existence,
in caring for and nurturing each of them.
All her children are made anew with cherished memories,
and tales of encouragement as they develop into their own
identities. Strengthening ten folds as they venture out
on their own.........."

Chapter 7

A sudden sensation causes me to stir and open my eyes pulling me from my slumber. My body is sheltered from the brightness of the sun. My vision was foggy, in my dozy state. Suddenly realizing I must have drifted off into a dreamland existence. Rubbing the sleep from my eyes, my vision now becomes clearer. Mackie is standing in front of me creating a huge shadow over my curled frame.

Adjusting my body to a sitting position saying, *"I must have fallen asleep."*

"Yes, I noticed, you drift off some time ago," continuing he says; *"the crew is stopping to have something to eat. Would you like to join us?"*

Rising I adjusted my attire, and say, *"I would love to."*

Grabbing my satchel, I follow him as he moves toward the edge of the wharf. I suddenly stop, and inquired, *"Where are we going?"*

Reaching the last crate, he turns to say; *"Follow me."* As we manouver around the wooden boxes I was surprised to find a secluded area behind a wall of shipping crates. Perfectly seclude on three sides, the fourth side facing the bay. It reminded me of a large room with one wall missing for a perfect view of the open waters. A nicely secluded gathered area, where several makeshift sleeping arrangements were distributed upon the worn deck boards.

Mackie says, *"The ship's cook has a meal prepared for the crew, you are welcome to join us."* As I watch the other dock workers heading behind a stack of crates.

Taking my hand in his, we start to follow the other workers. I came to an abrupt stop causing Mackie to halt his movement before we reached the edge of the dock that led to the clearing behind the wall of crates.

"Is there something wrong?" he inquires.

"No, I just feel bad you are inviting me for a meal. Can we invite the piper? He is trying to raise funds for the trip to New Scotland. He has no spare funds to purchase food, nor does he know anyone in the area. Can we ask him to join us? Do you think the cook will have enough to feed one more person? If not, I can share what I have in the sack that I brought from home? Please, we need to help him."

"Absolutely you stay here, I will go and invite him." As he quickly turns walking away, I say *"His name is William MacKay."*

I leaned against the large wooden wall of boxes, watching as Mackie spoke with the piper. Taking only a few minutes my vision observes the piper as he reaches down to pick up his sack and small tin cup that held his few coins. Watching them as they approach, these two tall strong men could be brothers. Similar in height and build. Their facial features are strong and handsome. Walking towards me both focus on me. William, carrying his Bag Pipes over his shoulder with a beaming smile on his face.

Approaching, he turns to say. *"Thanks, Maddie, for thinking of me. You are a kind lass."*

I look up at him and say, *"Because I arrived here alone, I appreciated being invited by Mackie. And thought why not add one more friend to share a meal with? We have all come together because of ship Hector, and new beginnings. Come I am sure between all of us we can scrape up enough to feed you as well."*

Mackie walks over to my side, taking my hand. He led me towards the private sheltered area behind a stack of crates. He introduces William and me to the rest of his crew.

He then led me to a pair of small wooden boxes that stood side by side. Informing me to sit and that he would be right back with our meals.

He was gone before I could inform him, I had my own food in my satchel. He soon returned carrying two wooden plates in one hand and two drinking mugs made of pewter in the other.

Stepping closer to where I sat, I quickly rose to assist him with his juggling act. Taking the two mugs filled with ale. With his free hand, he quickly grabbed the second plate. We sat on the crates with our backs resting against two larger wooden storage boxes.

Placing my cup of ale on the dock. I then picked up the small piece of Bannock that rested on my plate, alongside a scoop of corn and green beans. The Bannock was fresh and still warm. A bowl-shaped spoon sat on the plate beside a small mound of mashed black pudding. Devouring a spoonful of the warm pudding. I was famished and had not eaten since the break of dawn earlier that morning. Devouring my meal, as if it would be my last. My cup of ale was almost empty as I drank each tasty mouthful.

Mackie turns saying; *"You were hungry."*

Feeling more comfortable being in his presents. I turned to face him and reply; *"Famished, I had not eaten since breakfast, this morning. Thank you for inviting me, this was delicious. I am so grateful you asked me to join you, and your friends."*

"Would you like to have more? I can see if the cook has anything left?" he replied, as he started to rise from his sitting position.

I placed my hand gently on his arm, stopping him from rising, and say, *"No. this was wonderful. I am quite satisfied. If you show me where the galley is I can take these and get them cleaned up."*

"That won't be necessary the cook has a helper who takes care of all that." he passes both our plates to one of his workers as the dock worker walks in front of us.

"But I must work for my share!"

He nodded to the co-worker who took our cups, plates, and cutlery. Turning his vision back to mine, saying; *"Not today, you are my guest, tell me more about yourself. You told me you were a teacher."*

"Well, not quite," my vision down cast watching my fingers as they fumbled with the bottom of my apron. *"I only taught my siblings. When the Fraser family arrives on board, that is when my teaching skills will show. I am not sure how good I will be."* embarrassed to raise my eyes.

"I am sure you'll be just fine; I saw you reading earlier before you drifted off into a deep slumber. What were you reading?"

Nervous, still fussing with the apron over my smock. Embarrassed that he caught me dozing in my repose. I sheepishly replied; *"Sonnets by William Shakespeare. I especially like his second sonnet it reminds me of my mother."*

Chapter 8

The talk of reading the works of my favourite author had provided me with the courage to raise my vision to look upon his face. Sensing he also had the same passion.

He quickly stirred in his sitting position saying, *"I as well love reading his sonnets, his plays, and poems."* Taking a quick breath he continues, saying. *"My favourite is number eighteen."*

He quickly stood and moves to a stack of crates. Scaling them to the very top, He stood three large crates high. Standing like a statue his left hand outstretched towards the clouds, his right hand he places over his heart. Turning his vision to focus on my deep brown eyes, in a loud tenor voice he recites.

"Shall I compare thee to a summer's day?
Thou art more lovely and more temperate:
Rough winds do shake the darling buds of May,
And summer's lease hath all too short a date:
Sometimes too hot the eye of heaven shines,
And often is his gold complexion dimmed,
And every fair from fair sometime declines,
By chance, or nature's changing course untrimmed:
But thy eternal summer shall not fade,
Nor lose possession of that fair thou ow'st,
Nor shall death brag thou wand'rest in his shade,
When in eternal lines to time thou grow'st,
So long as men can breathe or eyes can see,
So long lives this, and this gives life to thee."

These loving words, translated over time:

"Shall I compare you to a summer's day?
You are more lovely and most modest.
Harsh winds blow disturbing the delicate buds of May,
our summers do not last long enough.
Sometimes the sun is too hot,
and your golden face is often dimmed by the clouds.
This is true all beautiful things become less beautiful,
of life's experiences or just by the passing of time.
However, your eternal beauty will never fade,
nor its qualities.
You will never die because you live forever,
and reside in my words of poetry.
If there are people alive to read these poems
this sonnet will live and you with it."

Concluding his professional performance, a rendition of this historical sonnet. Mackie jumps down to the wharf's wide plank boards. He gives a professional bow for his theatrical pose. Witnessing first-hand, his loud voice echoes out one of Shakespeare's most favourite sonnets.

Loud applauses, along with hoots and howls came from his shipmates, as well as me and the piper.

I sat captivated by his emotional rendition of this historical poem. My body tingled with emotions I had never experienced. My heart was beating way too fast. The palms of my hands clutched so tightly, trying to control these strange sensations my body was confronted with.

Concluding his theatrical rendition, He stood with feet placed equal to his broad shoulders, his hand still placed over his heart. He bent to waist high in a professional bow, his eyes never leaving my trans-fixated ones.

Unable to move, his piercing blue eyes captured mine in a hypnotic way. Sensing a message had been sent to me through these precious words he spoke. Delightful, touching, words meant only for me.

I sat frozen as he walks over, ever so slowly toward where I was sitting on the shipping crate. Standing before me, he reaches, garbing me gently under both my arms causing them to move over his shoulders. Our vision still focused on each other in a hypnotized emotion. His captivating blue eyes only focused on my hazy ones.

He picks me up and hugs me closer to his strong frame and spins me around, whispering in my ear. *"Did you feel that did you?"*

Startled by his inquiry, I did not quite know what to say, because I did feel something. Strange emotional sensations drifted over my slender physique, something I had never experienced before.

"Please tell me you felt it too?" he says, still slowly swinging me around.

All I could do was bury my head into the crevice of his neck and move my head in slow approval.

He immediately sensed my acceptance. Squeezing me a little tighter whispering so only I hear his low whisper. *"Shakespeare's sonnet eighteen has brought us together."*

Slowing our spinning bodies, to a stop. Then gently lowering me so my feet could touch the worn deck boards. Before releasing me, another strange sensation enveloped my small frame. As his lips placed the softest of feather-like peck just below my ear lobe. Sending strange tantalizing, sensations to parts of my emotionally aroused body. I never dreamed could be so overwhelming and comforting. Our hearts racing, thumping, beat for beat as he held me in his gentle embrace.

"I don't want to let you go," he whispered softly into my ear.

Startled, that I was reacting the same. Possibly, feeling so comfortable in his embrace, not wanting to break from these new strange, emotions, my body was experiencing.

Before I could say anything or reply, his shipmates pulled him away from our embrace.

Tapping him on the back, shouting as they encouraged him to have another pint of ale after such a wonderful performance. Congratulating him on his rendition of this famous sonnet written by Shakespeare and published over a century before.

He turns, and our eyes meet. Sending untold messages across the short distance between us. That only two emotional individuals could understand. Sensing what we had both just experienced was a beginning.

The beginning of what? I wondered.

This magnetic connection left me bewildered and unsettled. Unable to break from the visual pulls of his hypnotic blue eyes.

These strange emotions and sensations were running through my body. Afraid I would fall in a puddle on the weather-worn dock planks. All because of the weakened sensations, which were tingling over my small physique.

Quickly realizing I need to find something for support. Our visual connection remained strong. My vision fixated on his vision; I reached back confident there was a shipping box within my reach. My fingers tip touching its thick wooden surface. I slowly took one step back. The heel of my shoe slid along its side. My eyes remained transfixed on his. I slowly moved my other foot. My back was now able to rest against the high wooden wall of crates. Relieved for its support.

I release the breath I had been holding. Now confident, I avoided making an embarrassing show in front of the small group of his shipmates.

A message from his twinkling eyes, as his lips slightly curved into a small smile just as he was pulled away by his work friends. Our magnetic emotional connection was now broken.

Chapter 9

Turning my vision to the Dutch Whaler, which sits anchored in the harbour. Wondering how much longer it was going to take to move all these crates onto the vessel and store them below in the hole of the ship called Hector.

Reading the dark charcoal markings on the surrounding wooden boxes. So many of them revealed various clan names. Scanning them I read, MacGregor. MacKay, Robertson, MacDonald, another I spotted in the distant read, MacFarlane.

Realizing it must be their personal possessions. To my right, barrels were marked with the same black coal scribbles. These read, fresh drinking water. The markings on others were Tattie (Potatoes) carrots and Neeps, aka turnips.

There were many others to my left. Scanning these, they

had the same black coal markings that read "with a salt brine beef, mutton, or pork."

Over to the water's edge, I noticed a pile of woven sacks bursting at the seams. Strolling over to investigate with what they were filled. A sewn white woven cloth was attached to each sack. From the large pile several read, Smoked beef, smoked mutton, and curried cheese. One read dried beans, another read Sweetener; on another, I read, wild garlic, (for seasons.)

Looking over at the large stockpile of crates as well as the pile of sacks. I wondered; how long would it take the crew to move these bulky items. To get them uploaded onto the sailing vessel that was anchored in the bay.

These bulky shipping boxes were filled with an abundance of food to feed the crew and passengers during our month-long journey across the vast ocean.

Watching, as another ample collection was being placed on a floating platform to be hauled out and loaded aboard the ship Hector. Two workers were on another floating platform, this one was empty the two workers pushing it with large pools back to the wharf for another load.

I took my leave as the men started moving the crates in the area I had been sitting. I strolled over to the spot I originally sat beside the performing Piper.

He was nowhere to be seen. I sat took out one of my novels and proceeded to read. A loud shout came from Mackie as he approached my perch. Behind him was William MacKay the Piper.

"Am I OK to remain here?" I inquired as Mackie stood before me.

"Yes, these will be the last to be loaded." Continuing, *"I am sorry I needed to leave your side, we just got word the captain wishes to leave the day after tomorrow at daybreak. He has informed us*

that this calm weather will only last one more day at the most. The Capitan has been watching the tides and is confident the waters in the bay will still be at high tide that morning. We have a busy day before us to get all these crates, cartons, and barrels on the ship by nightfall tomorrow evening."

William the piper spoke; *"I have offered my services to help Mackie and the other dock workers with their task. They have so much to do, in such a brief time. If I help, the captain might provide me passage to board his ship for the new world."*

"What a wonderful idea." That was my reply.

"Can I entrust my pipes and travel bag in your care, while I work?" He inquires.

"Absolutely, I am pleased to help in any way, especially if it helps you gain passage and join us on the voyage."

Reaching for his satchel and pipes, he places them alongside my travel bags.

William leans close to me placing a feather peck on my cheek, whispering, *"You are so kind, thank you."*

As he turns to leave, Mackie lowers to whisper in my ear, *"You are a precious flower that has come into my life. Stay here while we hasten to get these cartons and barrels loaded on the ship."* Placing another one of his feather kisses below my ear.

Chapter 10

A novel on my lap, as I watch the parade of supplies being removed from the dock onto the barge and then ferried by the floating skiff onto the ship. This unremitting process became a rhythmic performance. The workers sing Olde ballads of Scottish folk tunes.

Resting my head against a large crate. I listen to their loud melodies drifting into the late afternoon sky as they worked tirelessly.

In their Scottish brogue, I hear a crew member singing in a beautiful baritone voice. _"Hey, Johnie Cope, are ye wauking yet?"_ Followed by a chorus of blended tones drifting over the water as the chorus of voices rose in harmony.

Somewhere in the distance, I hear a high tenor voice

from a young crew member I hear his beautiful voice blending seamlessly with the average baritone melodies from all the others.

In the dead silence when they finish their song, another sailor yells, *"Came ye o'er frae France."* And the chorus of male tones drifts over the valley.

Every so often during one of their Scottish songs a low bass sound drifts over the still waters of the bay.

Working so tediously to get as many cartons as possible and sacks loaded onto ship Hector. I hear these beautiful folk songs. I sat with my eyes closed, my back resting against a crate. Allowing their harmonized sweet melodies to envelop my small frame.

A loud cry from a crew member aboard the ship who yells, *"Let us sing "Black Joke."*

A roar of laughter from all the workers drifting from the ship, across the skiffs, to the crew on the wharf. In the chorus, I hear, *"Her black yoke and belly so white...."*

Laughing to myself knowing the meaning of these words from this old Scottish folk song. They worked late into the evening with the light of a full moon.

The clanging of a dinner bell brought everyone to attention. The last barge was uploaded onto the ship and placed on the vessel. These last two loads would remain on the deck of the ship until the first light. The crew working in the hull below found it too dark to manoeuvre these last few large crates into place. The remaining shipping packages would have to wait till morning when the sun rose. The dimness of the evening drifting over the bay made it difficult for their rhythmic process to continue.

Mackie and William both tall and broad across the shoulders approached. Walking towards me like two long-lost brothers, who had not seen each other for many a year.

Both were bare-chested, water droplets falling from their long wavy locks. Mackies' black tresses hung down over his barely clad broad chest.

Striding alongside in joking merriment Williams' wavy light brown tresses also dripping with gleaming wetness. Their britches clung to their large broad thighs, dripping water onto the wharf, and leaving a wet pathway of footprints on the large planks. Both were bare-chested, ringing the water from their white tunics.

I notice the remaining crew members had also taken a dip into the bay to remove the sticky sweaty droplets from their strong muscular frames, as they entered our private shelter quarters. Both men were dripping in water.

Mackie walked towards me. The toes of his boots touched the crate I sat on. He leans down placing his large palms on the crate beside my hips. His face was level with mine. Drip, drip from the ends of his long curly black locks falling over my slender frame. His piercing blue eyes look far too mischievously into my deep brown ones. His lips turn to a smile, then suddenly he shakes his head like a wet dog spraying me with rapid droplets of salty sea water over my physique.

The shock of his playful trick has me pushing him away from the cool wet moisture that is now covering my body. I hear Williams's deep howls as he gives Mackie a shove on the shoulder. Saying *"Mackie you are full of devilment, what a wretched thing to do to this lovely lass."*

Mackie leans in and whispers in my ear, *"Now we are wet together my lass,"* as he places a tender peck on the nape of my neck.

His touch sends alarming sensations through my small frame. I push him away saying, *"The chef has our evening meal ready, let's go and eat."*

William quickly interjects saying; *"I'll go get our meals, you two say here."*

Mackie lowers to the crate beside me his wet thigh pressing against my leg. The dampness from his britches is seeping thru my smock. I feel the heat from his thigh through the damp fabric separating our bodies. This man knows how to arouse these strange sensations that run through my small physique whenever he touches me. These strange emotions racing all over my frame that only he has the power to activate.

Mackie quickly grabs me and brings me into a tender embrace, apologizing for his playful trick. I push him away saying; *"You are wicked, you have me soaked to the bone with your wetness."*

His broad arms encase my body closer to his damp frame and whispers in my ear. *"I love how your breast reacts to the cool damp water. They rise, perk to attention. Wanting to be suckled."*

"You are wicked!" I softly reply.

"But you love when I tease you, do you not?"

Embarrassed by his inquiry, not sure how I should respond. Never had this form of tantalizing reaction envelope my young female stature before. However, not want him to stop these enthusiastic seductive overtures.

Before I could reply, he softly murmurs; *"Tell me to stop and I will."*

All I could do was shake my head indicating I did not want him to ever stop.

He brings me tighter into his embrace, and whispers, *"I have fallen in love with you sweet maiden."*

Not having a response.

I hear Williams's loud voice saying, *"I have our evening meals and mugs of ale."*

As Mackie releases me, he places another one of his tender kisses below my ear lobe.

Sitting on my crate surrounded by a large gathering of male workers. Feeling so shy being the only female among the crowd of bare-chested men.

Until I arrived at the wharf, the only man I had ever seen bare-chested was my father. Viewing the large group of bare-clad workers. I noticed the elder men's chests were covered with large masses of chest hair. Whereas the younger men had little if no hairs on their bare chests. Turning my vision to William and Mackie who sat close to me. I scanned their bare bodies noticing they had a little more than the younger ones. However, not as much as the older men.

Mackie leans down and whispers, *"Does looking at a man's bare body bother you? I can ask them to put their tunics back on."*

I place my right hand on his and softly say. *"No, it does not bother me. I was just scanning the workers."*

He reaches for my empty plate, placing it with his. Standing he thanks William for obtaining our meal, and says, *"Maddie and I are going for a walk along the boardwalk, can you look after our dinner plate."*

"Sure mate;" He turns his attention to me saying; *"Enjoy your evening stroll, Maddie."*

Mackie raises his left arm over my shoulder, steering me away from the secluded shelter, lit only by the small fire in the cooking chamber.

"We accomplished quite a lot today, loading these cartons onto the ship. I was informed tomorrow's workload would not be as tedious."

"That's good," I say with a soft whisper.

"I'm told Reverend James Robertson will be holding a service for the departing passengers before we board the ship for our journey across the vast waters."

"Will the service be held tomorrow?" I inquire.

"No, the day after. Tomorrow will be another day like today." Continuing, he says, *"Our task will take us until dusk again tomorrow."*

Continues saying; *"Captain Spiers wishes to depart with first light at high tide the following day."*

Walking in the shadows of the glowing full moon we reach the end of the wharf.

He guides me towards a wall of the last business establishment. Turning me to face him, his large hands rise to gently bring my face to his for a tender kiss. His lips slowly slide over my small, closed ones.

I raise my arms to encase them around his neck keeping his tender lips against mine. His tantalizing movement is sending arousing sensations rushing throughout my petite physique.

His embrace slightly increases bringing me tighter into his comforting arms. His right leg was placed between my legs pressing gently against my lower region. I feel his hardened member against my right thigh. I wither against him, unsure of these emotions that are rushing thru my small frame.

This man envelops my body with beautiful emotions. Never wanting to cease from these aroused stimulations that are dangerously thrilling.

Is this what the feeling of love, is like I wonder?

His rapid breathing and heart rate is matching mine, emotions running through both our bodies as our mouths duel like two demanding lovers.

He parts from my lips his forehead leaning against mine. My breathing grew, raspy and rapid. His matching mine with the same emotions.

In Gaelic he whispers *"tha gaol agam ort"* (translated, *"I Love you"*), continuing as he pulls me into his embrace saying;

"gaol mo chridhe" (Love of my heart.) he whispers in my ear.

Tears fall from my eyes caused by his tender words. These emotions he has unearthed from my small frame, are alarming yet so welcoming. Never wanting them to come to an end, nor wanting to leave his comforting embrace. Feeling so emotionally connected to him.

He gently pulls from our emotional cuddle, placing his large hands on my cheeks wiping the tears that are falling.

"Why are you crying, my love? Did I harm or offend you?"

"No," I quickly respond as I bring my small hands to wrap around his large ones.

Continuing. *"Your comforting embrace. Your, passionate kisses, and tender words, are so touching. My heart swells when I am in your comforting arms. My entire body rushes with strange sensations from your enthusiastic kisses and tender loving words. If this is what happens when someone falls in love then, I as well Love you."*

Chapter 11

The morning of departure has finally arrived. I lay curled up on the wharf snuggled in a wool blanket. Mackie had retrieved them for us last evening from the hole of the ship. My vision focuses on the sun as it starts to rise from its watery grave in the eastern sky. Rising my head, I am alerted by the loud nasal sounds from William as he sleeps soundly a few feet to my right. Another male's loud sleeping snorts bring my attention to my back. Turning I witness Mackie sprawled on his back making blowhorn sounds from his nostril cavity.

I slowly rise and move amongst the other crew members who also chose to sleep on the old wharf last evening. I rise and wander to the end of the dark blank boards where the privy was located. After relieving myself I descended the makeshift ladder and follow a small path that leads beneath the wharf. The tide is high and still rising. However, looking toward the water lines, I would say the outgoing tide would start reseeding around mid-day.

Reaching a secluded spot under the cover of the wharf. I quickly remove my night dress and lower my naked form into the cool refreshing water under the covered deck boards. With my small nappy in hand, I give my slender frame a quick bath. Rushing to complete my bathing before the crew members woke from their night's slumber.

I lower my naked frame for a quick refreshing dip. Leaving the refreshingly cool water, I quickly gather my night dress to use it to dry the moisture from my slender frame. I promptly reach for one of my clean smocks from my travel satchel. Slide it over my head just as I hear Mackie's distressed voice.

"Maddie, where are you? William, have you seen Maddie?"

William's dozy response, *"What did you say, Mackie....what's wrong?"*

"Maddie's gone; do you know where she has disappeared to? She is not here; her satchel is also gone!" I hear Mackies frightened cries above me.

"What? Why would she leave?" William inquires.

Completing my feminine hygiene. I rinse my hair, drying the excess moisture with my nightdress. I hear the commotion of the entire crew as they scurry above me. Mackie has everyone rushing around to try and find where I had gone to.

Recognizing his distressing loud voice as he calls my name. I quickly leave the sheltered confines beneath the wharf, making my way to the clearing at the end of the landing. Reaching the ladder that would take me back up to the deck boards. Raising my right foot to the bottom board I hear.

"Mackie here she is!" The male voice shouts coming from

above startles me. I turn my vision to the shipmate who was looking down at me.

Hearing an urgent rush of heavy footsteps running along the wooden deck boards above me. From the corner of my eye, I see the movement of a male as he flies from the dock into the shallow low water beside me.

I instantly froze as both my feet came to rest on the bottom rung ready to climb. Mackie rushes to my side removing me from the ladder and into his large embrace. His breathing rushes as he buries his face into the crevice of my neck. Softly saying, *"You gave me such a fright, I thought you left, why did you leave and not tell me?"*

"You were deep in slumber, and I needed to bathe in private before the ship departs," I replied as I wrapped my arms around his large muscular frame.

"You should have woken me; I could have guarded the area in case one of my shipmates decided to disturb your bathing."

"You, along with William and the crew were deep in sleep. So, I took advantage of this early morning sunrise to sneak below under the wharf to bathe in private."

"You smell like a fresh flower garden in spring." He whispers as he snuggles into my neck. Placing a small peck below my right ear.

A commotion from above takes us out of our tender embrace.

A deep male voice could be heard bellowing questions.

Mackie quickly releases me, helping me to ascend the homemade ladder.

Landing on the deck boards Mackie quickly leaves my side and rushes towards the loud masculine voice. The vision of Captain Spier appears just as Mackie reaches the middle of the wharf. The two walk together heading to a stack of crates that had arrived late last evening.

"What are these cates doing on the wharf?" The Capitan sternly inquires.

"They must have arrived during the night or early this morning. The crew and I worked late into the night to ensure the wharf was cleared of all cartons and crates before we rested for our nights' slumber."

A ruckus drew the captain's and Mackie's attention to turn. Passengers were descending to the wharf pushing carts containing, crates and large wrappings of their personal items.

"What is this?" The captain inquires.

"Gather the crew to move these items below deck. I want to depart as soon as the vessel is loaded." The captain says as he quickly leaves Mackie's side in a huff.

Mackie quickly directs the crew to have all these newly arrived shipping cartons and crates loaded aboard the vessel as quickly as possible.

My vision suddenly spotted Laird and Lady Fraser among the arriving passengers. I rush in their direction to greet them. Lady Fraser is holding her youngest Samuel in her arms. Their two other children Sarah and Matthew were sitting on top of a small wooden cart, loaded with their family possessions.

"This must be Samuel." Bringing him into my embrace. I quickly turn my attention to the other two children.

Ruffling the dark curly locks of the young boy saying, *"You my dear must be Matthew!"*

He looks up at me with a large grin on his face.

Turning to the young girl, *"You must be their big sister. Am I right?"*

She nods her head with a big smile on her face shaking in acknowledgement.

"My name is Maddie, and I'm so pleased to meet you all."

Lady Fraser takes me into a gentle hug, *"I am so glad you're here; the children have been impatient to meet you. We told them all about you joining us on this journey."*

Laird Fraser lowers the handles of the small cart, also taking me into a comforting embrace, saying. *"Welcome to our family, I'm so glad to see you here."*

Releasing me he continues, *"The children were excited to see you as well. We told them all about you, they could not wait until we arrived at the wharf."*

Lord Fraser's left arm still resting over my shoulder. From the corner of my vision, I witnessed Mackie briskly walking toward our small family gathering.

Arriving on my right, he extends his hand towards the Laird, saying; *"You must be Lord Fraser. Maddie has told me so much about you. I am Malcolm Lyon; however, everyone calls me Mackie."*

Continuing. He says, *"I'm surprised you and your family chose to leave your Estate in the Highlands and venture on this long journey to unknown lands across the vast ocean."*

The Laird quickly replies, *"It's a pleasure to me you Mackie, this is my wife, Lady Fraser."*

Mackie turns, taking Lady Frasers' right hand, saying. *"It's a pleasure to me you, my lady."* Holding her small hand in his, he bows at the waist placing a delicate peck on the back of her hand.

The Laird says, *"My wife is holding Samuel our youngest."* He then places his hand on the back of his middle child saying, *"This is Matthew."* Continued as he ruffles the blonde curls of his daughter saying, *"This wee lass is Sarah, our oldest."*

Mackie quickly gathers Sarah in his broad arms saying, *"You are so beautiful, we should be calling you Princess Sarah."*

She shyly giggles as she hides her face into the nape of his broad neck.

Laird Fraser quickly gathers Matthew into his arms. As we step to the side so the crew members approaching could take the cart and roll it towards the end of the pier where the large net was being lowered onto the barge below.

The Laird turns to Mackie saying, *"I am the youngest male in the Fraser Family. I have no wish to be Lord of the Kindail Estate, or any other for that matter. My dreams are only for my wife and family."*

He reaches for his wife's hand takes it to his lips and places a tender kiss on the back of her hand.

He continues, saying, *"Our only interest is to start a new life with our young family in this faraway country called New Scotland. My oldest brother holds the title to our family Kindail Estate."*

The shout from the crew workers moving the crates, calls for Mackie's help.

He leans in places a kiss on my cheek and says, *"I must go and help load these many boxes and crates, I will meet up with you later."* As he rushes off to help his workmates get the final items loaded onto the ship.

We suddenly hear the ringing of the church bells. Alerting us that the small service was about to begin at the local parish church in town.

Chapter 12

Pending the departure of the ship Hector. The aging Reverend James Robertson also known as "The Mighty Minister," turns to his congregation and the surrounding areas of the Scottish Highlands. Welcoming the large gathering. The service was held in the Courtyard, alongside his small white chapel in Loch Broom. His Church was far too small to hold this large congregation. Consisting, of the departing passengers, and their loved ones who came to wish them farewell.

He held an open-air communion service and prayers to bless these travellers. Who would board Ship Hector on their voyage to New Scotland across the vast ocean waters?

A soft warm rainfall fell over the congregation blending with the salty tears that flowed down their cheeks.

We stood among the crowd of passengers, and well-wishers. Laird and Lady Fraser and I were holding the three Children.

The service was well underway when Mackie and William appeared. Each took one of the Fraser children from our arms. Mackie took Sarah placing her over his shoulders so she could have a bird's eye view of this emotional prayer service. William took Matthew following the same process, lifting the young lad, and placing him on his shoulders. Laird Fraser embraced his youngest in his arms.

The two children resting on the two tall men's shoulders giggled as they sat so high looking over the massive crowd that stood solemn.

A saddened hush fell over the passengers and their family members during this memorable service. The communion prayer took longer than the ship's Captain had expected. Delaying the departure of the sailing vessel leaving later that morning in July than he had anticipated. He was hoping to depart early in the morning with the receding high tide.

Adding to Hectors' delay was the process of rowing the many passengers a few at a time along with their sacks and remaining wooden crates containing their possessions. Items they were allowed to take aboard for their long journey. Causing a frustrating delay in the captain's departure time.

The last of the passengers were now being rowed out to the waiting ship.

Piper: William MacKay stood at the edge of the wharf waiting with his bagpipes in a ready stance to perform for the departing vessel and its passengers.

Mackie and the crew who had worked tediously to load the many supplies, approached the captain informing him how helpful Piper MacKay was over the last few days. They were certain without his assistance they would never have completed their task of loading the large crates and barrels on time.

Captain Spier stood waiting until the very last passenger was aboard ship Hector. Before deciding to allow the Piper MacKay from Sutherlandshire to board the vessel and accompany them on their journey.

The weighted anchor of the Dutch Built Ship called Hector was raised. Her massive sails lowered and bellowed with the light wind that blew out of Loch Broom harbour. The weather was misty as they gathered around the edges of the large vessel waving goodbye to their friends, family, and homeland.

Piper MacKay dressed in his Plaid from his family heritage. Stood on the bow of the ship and played "We shall return no More" as the ship headed out of the bay into the open seas.

On that memorable mid-Summer day, of July 1773 the "Hector" slowly drifted out of Loch Broom with Highlander emigrants. Twenty-Three families, Twenty-Five single men. All hoping for a much better life in New Scotland.

Chapter 13

We were directed to stay in the water-tight compartment below the ship in the dark cavern with no window, only allowed to come up the short flight of stairs for meals and when Ship Hector sailed in calm seas. Other than those times we were confined to the hull of the vessel in rough waters.

The ship Hector travelled across the wide ocean moving at a slow sail of five to six knots. On sunny calm days, we quickly rose from the dark hole of the vessel. Climbing up from the stench of vomit and urine that hung in the closed confinement below deck. Cherishing the rays of sunshine and warm breeze as we sat out in the open listening to tales and stories from the many Scottish companions, who shared these small spaces with us.

Our first meal was Oat Bread and Barley soup. We would line up with wooden bowl-shaped plates and a jug for a pint of water. The shipmates doled our daily rations. Our weekly food consumption was three pounds of salt beef, four pounds of bread, and four pounds of oatmeal. I helped the other ladies of the ship taking turns collaborating with the onboard cook and helping to feed the over two hundred passengers and crew. Our cooking stoves were metal-sand boxes secured to the ship and filled with sand, over a small fire in the center of the sand.

Reaching our tenth day at sea, we were restricted below deck since we had departed Lock Broom, as the ship sailed into ruff stormy weather. The young children became restless because of the restrictions of remaining in their bunks, in the darkness for so long.

Gathering several of my children's books, I say; *"Who would like to hear a story?"*

They quickly jump from their enclosed sleeping quarters in our steerage compartment and gather around my bunk.

"OK, let us go up on deck, where it is sunny and warm, the sun just peaked out from behind the clouds. Come follow me.

I sat at the bow of the vessel facing a large gathering of passengers, the smallest of the children sat closest to me. Midship their parents and a large gathering of the crew, sat facing me to hear my reading. The book I chose was *"The Glass Slipper"* also known as *"Cinderella."* All sat captivated as I read with emotions enhancing the dramatic areas. Overwhelmed to witness the hypnotic eyes of the little ones who sat enthralled by my storytelling. *"The end"*

Barely getting these words out of my mouth, the crowd of children shouted, *"Read us another."* Reaching in my sack I pull another story by the same author.

Adjusting my seating position, I spot Mackie on the starboard side of the ship, behind the seated, parents. He was leaning against the outer rail of the vessel his blue eyes fixated on mine, with a large smile on his face. My vision focused on his strong facial features, unable to disconnect from the grip he has on me. He brings two fingers to his lips, placing a kiss on the tips. Blowing the tender kiss towards me with a wink of his eye and a broad smile. Startled by this affectionate and tender de-meaner, I re-adjust my sitting position, aroused by his erotic overture.

The small voices of young children brought me out of my awe-struck behaviour The next book I held in my hand to read was *"The Master Cat,"* Adventures of <u>Puss in Boots</u>.

Reading the last line, *"Puss became a great Lord and never ran after the mice again. Except in playful diversion."* Closing the book just as a drop of rain fell on its black cover.

Finishing my renditions, I rest my back against the boards of the ship, my vision focusing on the piper. William MacKay unlimbered his bagpipes and proceeded to play a familiar Scottish tune. A large group of passengers danced along the wooden deck. Twirling young children in their arms. The young men playfully wrestled for entertainment. Others gather for a card game or two. Several others just sat and shares tales of their homeland.

The captain rose on a platform to address the large gathering of passengers, saying. *"This is a gentle warm rainfall we are sailing thru. I suggest we divide the ship into two sections with sail cloth draped between them. The woman and young children can bath under the soft rainfall on the port side of the ship, and the men will take the aft section."* Continued, saying; *"We should take advantage of the gentle rain to refreshen our bodies."*

Motioning to the crew to place the large sails dividing the vessel into two sections. The ladies hurried to the hull to gather a change of clothing. Returning with a container of their homemade, Lye-based soap. We worked quickly taking advantage of this warm shower to bathe the young ones, then ourselves.

Chapter 14

Assisting Lady Fraser with her three young children. Once they were fully scrubbed and clothed. I quickly slipped down to my chemise and promptly took advantage of the soft rainfall cleansing my small frame. I reach into my carpet bag pulling out another chemise, this one was created from an opaque fabric, smocked with red dyed yarn across the bosom. Creating a fully gathered garment from my midriff to below my knees.

Lady Fraser gathers her children taking them below out of the falling raindrops. I proceeded to gather all the garments, washing them with a large bar of lye soap. Laying them down on the deck of the ship for the soft rain to rinse off the excess washing powder. Mackie appeared with two wooden buckets. Both were full of rainwater he collected from the rolled-up sails.

I quickly gathered the children's items of clothing and dunked them one at a time into the bucket. Quickly pulling them back out to ring the moisture out.

Mackie sat beside me, clad only in his breeches, saying; *"You rinse the garments, and I will wring out the water. Together we can get the job done faster."* He quickly completed the children's garments. In one hand he held my chemise in the other Lady Fraser's garment. I quickly reach over to remove them from his fingers when he placed them behind his back.

"What are you doing?" I inquire. Puzzled by his playful behaviour.

"You pick the hand that holds Lady Fraser, and I will give you both of them." He looks at me with those playful blue eyes of his, then continues; *"If you pick wrong then you only get Lady Fraser."*

"No, you can't do that, I need my garment back I only brought two with me."

"You will get it back, but only at a time of my choosing."

"Why do you want to keep my chemise?"

"Just because," then leans closer to me and whispers, *"You haunt my dreams, and I need something of yours to ease my wonderment."*

"Why do you suffer such restlessness?"

Continuing in his soft whisper inches from my face, *"I have fallen in love with you, sweet maiden. Before I met you, I was feeling lost and alone. Drifting, not knowing where I was going or why. Since you walked into my life, I have a purpose, my life now has meaning."*

I choose the right hand hoping that was the one that held my garment. He does a quick shuffle revealing Lady Frasers' garment in his right hand.

I quickly say; *"You switched them, as I chose the right hand. Didn't you?"*

He looks at me with that boyish grin, saying. *"You were*

quick to catch my trick of deceptions." Passing me both garments. I lay them on the deck to dry from the heat of the sun.

He then leans in, taking both my hands in his, and places a tender kiss on my fingers saying, "*I know what I want. Where I want to go and whom I want to share it with. It is you and only you.*"

He then pulls me into his embrace placing a soft feather peck below my ear sending those tingling sensations rushing through me. Feeling dizzy from his affection, we slowly lower to settle on the deck. He pulls me onto his lap as he places his long slender fingers on my face and slowly brings my mouth to his. His lips slid gently along my closed ones teasing them.

My hands slide under his arms clasping together on his bare back.

I submit to his demanding affection for a passionate smooch. Unaware this is how lovers embrace when their lips meet for an enthusiastic kiss. My body is racing with strange sensual emotions, too new to react, but not wanting to depart from them.

I am melting in his comforting arms, as my scenes capture his manly scent of musk and cloves.

A strange fluttering sensation slowly moves over my small frame. My heart is racing. My breathing accelerated with the slow movements of his tongue. My mind is confused, with these raw emotions that are rushing to strange parts of my body. Never wanting to stop, or slow down.

Confused, I wonder what is happening, not wanting to leave his embrace nor put a halt to these strange loving overtures. My emotions are in a whirlwind.

These desires rush down my body to the sensitive area's that I never felt inflamed before. Nor have I experienced these tingling agitations from the buds of my nipple between my thin chemise and his bare physique.

My breast slowly pressing against his bare chest is escalating these feelings. A sudden tingling, twitching sensation over my nether region between my legs is heightened. But why?

Is this what being in love is? I wonder.

My head is in a foggy cloud, yet my body wants more. Not wanting these beautiful arousing tremors to stop.

The tipping rain is no longer falling. A rush of voices drifts around me. His body slowly moves from beneath my small frame.

Slowly, he releases his loving embrace, saying; *"Let's tend to the wet garments."*

Lifting me from his lap. He quickly rises bringing me into his tall frame and whispers, *"Are you feeling weak in the knees?"*

Leaning in his embrace, all I could do was shake my head in approval. My body felt feeble and shaky. My legs are like rubber, not wanting to cooperate. Nor provide me with the strength I require to stand upright.

"That's what love does; it makes you mopsy." As he places me to lean against the taffrail of the ship.

I watch as he quickly moves to gather my discarded wet garments from the bucket. Along with those of the Fraser family.

Lowering inches from me. Placing the damp items on the warm floor of the ship, he leans close to my left ear and whispers. *"I could spend all day in those loving arms of yours."*

Slowly turning his eyes fixated on mine, I shyly whisper, *"Me as well."* Embarrassed by my words, I lower my vision to the small hands that sat on my lap.

He gently places a finger under my chin, slowly rising my face to meet his. He leans closer placing another tender soft peck on my lips.

Slowly parting from our kiss, he whispers; *"Hector has brought us together, and you into my life, my love."*

Walking away leaving my body afire with sensual emotions. Wondering how I am ever going to control these strange sensations that he has provoked in my small frame.

Gathering the other family garments, I had laid earlier, he places them by my side. I am amazed there are only a few that still need to be laid on the deck to dry. My chemise was bone dry, along with many of the children's garments.

Placing the few damp articles back on the warm deck boards, I leave the bow of the ship. Approaching the staircase, which leads to the passenger sleeping compartment of the vessel. Before descending I turn to look back at Mackie as he again raised two fingers to his lips placing a tender kiss and then blows the floating peck in my direction.

Chapter 15

Descending, I arrive at the family Fraser bunks to find Lady Fraser in distress.

"What is the matter, my Lady?" I inquire.

"I'm feeling a bit unwell, can you tend to the children while I rest?"

"Absolutely, come children, follow me up to the deck and I'll read you another story," I say cradling baby Samuel into my arms. Directing Sarah age six, and Matthew age four to proceed ahead of me up the stairs, toward the sunny blue skies.

Proceeding towards the bow of the ship where I had left our remaining garments to dry.

Reaching the large deck boards, the two older children run off to the area of the ship where I often sat and read to them.

Feeling the heat of the sunshine envelope my small frame, I gently move baby Samuel to my other arm, just as Mackie comes up behind me, reaching to take the young barren from my arms.

Mackie stops, frozen in his tracks. I turn to see why he was not following me to the bow of the ship. He is pulling Samuel's small frame from his bare chest, saying; *"this wee bairn is afire."*

"What are you saying?" I inquire.

"He is burning with fever. Let us take him to the Kindred," (aka, a medical professional, or Doctor).

"I must go and inform the Laird and Lady Fraser, you take him to see the doctor," continuing. *"I'll make sure the other two are looked after."* Before I could leave Mackie gently takes my arm, saying; *"you best bring them along, they may be suffering from the same ailment."*

"What are you saying?" I say, startled by his comment.

"Just do as I say I'll explain everything later." he rushes toward the stern of the large vessel.

Hurriedly, I gather Sarah and Matthew, then scurry over to where the male passengers sat drinking ale and sharing tales.

Informing the laird of his wife's condition as well as his wee young ones.

Mackie and I hurry to the physician's, consulting cabin, located at the rear of the large vessel, next to the captain's quarters.

Lord Fraser carrying his daughter Sarah in his muscular arms, I held Matthew against my small frame.

The doctor's diagnosis was unsettling, advising Lord Fraser he needs to examine his wife immediately before he could divulge his professional diagnosis.

The two concerned men left the consulting quarters. The door was no sooner closed, and I turned to Mackie, *"What illness do they have?"* I inquire.

"I'm not sure," was Mackie's reply.

"*Please, you must know something, you are frightening me.*" I continued, inquiring, "*Tell me what alarmed you to rush the bairn to seek medical help?*"

"*Along with the fever, I noticed these red spots on the wee baby.*"

I quickly turned my attention to young Matthew, to see if he had the same red spots. Finding two on his back under his shirt.

Startled, I quickly say; "*I found two on his back. What does that mean?*"

Just then the doctor enters followed by the Laird, saying. "*It is confirmed we have an out brake of smallpox. We must immediately quarantine the infected passengers in a separate area.*"

Continuing he says, "*All passengers and crew aboard the vessel must be examined as quickly as possible!*"

My vision quickly turns to Mackie, all he could do was shake his head in approval. His prompt suspicions were correct.

All three Fraser children were examined. All showed signs of the contagious disease and would need to be segregated from the other passengers.

The doctor turns to Lord Fraser guiding him to the enclosed examination area, saying, "*You must be checked as well, my Lord.*" Directing him to enter the private curtain-off area.

Sitting in the small, confined cabin we hear the doctor's voice from behind the curtain. "*You can dress, I found none of the pustule's spot on your body,*" continuing, "*Your family will be placed in isolation.*"

"*I will be staying with my lady along with my children, they will be cared for by only me,*" he says, pulling up his suspenders as he exits the examining area.

"*Are you sure, my Lord?*" The doctor inquires, continuing he says; "*You could catch this deadly disease and possibly die.*"

"*I am sure,*" he replies, "*There is no life for me if my wife dies.*

Besides, she carries my child, and I will remain by her side, and those of my heirs."

Mackie was the next to be examined by the physician. He as well was clear of any spots.

As he stepped out from behind the cloth shield, he turns to the doctor saying, *"I will go and inform the Caption of your findings, and return."* He and Lord Fraser, gather the three children in their arms and walk out of the doctor's cabin.

I rose and entered the private examination area and disrobe. I stood; my arms wrapped around my naked frame. Only my mother saw my naked body. No male has ever seen my bare-clad slender frame, not even my father.

Reflecting on that thought, I wonder, he must have seen my bare body when I was a wee babe. Never had I exposed my bare-naked female form in front of any man.

Just then the Doctor, spoke from the other side of the white cloth wall, saying. *"There is no need to be shy, nor embarrassed of your body. I have seen many men and women unclothed. For me, when I look at a bare-clad body, it is for medical research nothing more. So please trust me,"* continuing, *"may I enter?"*

"Yes," I say, with barely a whisper.

He slides the white curtain aside and enters the private space. The back of my naked frame is facing him as he takes a step and enters.

"Maddie, are you still here?" Mackie says as we hear the creaking of the clinic door.

"Yes, the Doctor is just about to check my body for spots." I quickly respond, so relieved I would not be alone in the room with this male specialist. While he scans my small frame for those red pustular welts that appeared on the Fraser family.

His examination revealed no sign of pox marks on my

unclothed exposed frame. He promptly leaves the secluded area allowing me to dress and cover my naked body.

Finally clothed, I quickly slide the white curtain back and say, *"Am I OK to go now?"*

"Yes, your body showed no signs of any spots."

Mackie quickly grabs my hand and pulls me from the confined room. Placing a comforting arm over my shoulder. We leave, only to find the captain and the crew lined up down the narrow hall waiting to enter the Doctors' examination room to be checked for spots.

Chapter 16

My heart is racing from this shocking ordeal, I had little if no knowledge of this disease called "SMALLPOX."

Mackie quickly directs me towards the deck of the ship, into a blinding mid-day sunshine. Reaching the bow of the vessel we sat against the bulkhead. Pulling me into his comforting arms. I lean in close placing my head on his broad chest and hearing the beating of his heart. We sat in silence for a long time, contemplating this impending serious situation this vessel has encountered.

I finally spoke, *"I was so glad you came back to the Doctor's office when you did,"* slowing for a breath I continued, *"I was so frightened to be alone with him, you arrived just in time."*

"Did he hurt you?" He promptly inquires.

"No, nothing like that, I was afraid because I stood before him with no garments on. I have never disrobed in front of anyone before, I felt uneasy to do so before a man."

"I rushed back, wanting to make sure he found no red welts on your body." he continues saying. *"Did he check if you have a fever?"*

"Yes, no fever"

"We'll stick together and try to avoid as many passengers as we can."

William the Piper started walking towards us. Mackie, quickly rose his right hand, indicating for the piper to stop.

The piper froze saying, *"It's OK, the doctor has checked, and I have none of those red welts everyone is talking about."* Continuing, he inquires, *"Am I to assume you both have been cleared?"*

We both acknowledge we were Mackie raises his hand indicating William to come and join us.

"Maddie and I could still have some of the sticky pustular saliva. We held the ailing children in our arms when we carried the sick ones to the Doctor's clinic."

"How can we rid this sticky substance from your bodies?" the piper inquires.

"Not sure, we might start with salt water." was Mackie's reply. Continuing, *"I witnessed an elderly matron use it on a badly infected toe on a friend of mine. When the wrappings were removed, his toe was healed back to normal."*

William rose from the deck, to say; *"We have lots of saltwater surrounding this vessel, I'll run and grab as many buckets as I can find."*

Leaving my side, Mackie quickly rose to say; *"I'll notify the captain and gather the spooled lanyards."*

Captain Spiers was open to any recommendation that would help eradicate this deadly disease.

These pustules red spots, aches, and pains along with high fever could spread quickly if nothing was done. Knowing he had to quickly control this epidemic before it took hold of the entire sailing vessel. Having experienced these symptoms before. Aboard one of his other voyages to the Colonies to the south of New America.

He had never heard nor experienced the concept of dousing the passengers with buckets of salty seawater. However, the tale shared by Mackie certainly adds substance to this theory that it may help. It certainly would not hurt, nor harm anyone.

As a sea captain for many years, he experienced times when the swells were so high, they washed over the decks of Ship Hector. Dousing himself and his crew so many times.

Instructing his crew to gather all the buckets and follow William, the piper to retrieve buckets of salty seawater from the vast ocean below.

Captain Spiers, then turned towards the poop deck, going up the few risers to the quarterdeck. With Mackie's help, they placed a small wooden shipping container on the raised area of the floorboards of ship Hector. Mackie helps the captain to stand on top of the makeshift podium in a loud voice.

"Everyone listen up, we are going to try and control this devastating sickness. Everyone is required to be inspected by the Doctor. Following his inspection, if infected you will be taken to a segregated area below. If he deems, you are free of the red sores you are to return to the deck and a sailor will douse you with a bucket of salty water."

A ruck-us rose from the gathered passengers, as they shouted with alarming shock. None of them wished to have cold salt water poured over their bodies.

Mackie promptly climbed upon the crate to stand next to the captain, saying; *"I was the one who found the diseased spots on a young child. Rushing, I carried that ailing baby close to my bare chest."* Rising his both hands, placing them on his chest indicating where he once held the youngster. Continuing; *"If the saltwater removes the diseased pustules from my skin, preventing the disease from entering my body. I will be the first to stand and have my shipmate drench me with the salty brine."* He quickly steps down, and the crowd parts as he walks proudly to the bow of the ship where William stood waiting with a bucket of salty seawater.

My vision caught Mackie's broad smile as he averts his sight toward where I sat. Approaching he takes my hand in his massive palm. We both move towards William who is holding a wooden bucket. I was confident it was filled with that cold salty liquid.

Stopping in front of the piper. Mackie places his hand into the buck, ensuring his hands and arms would be covered with the cold liquid. Then turns his back to William giving me a smile as the first bucket was slowly raised over his head. William made sure the water fell upon the chest region, where the sickly child rested its delicate small frame.

Mackie steps aside, shaking his tall frame like a wet dog caught out in spring rainfall.

Dripping in chilly water he slowly approaches, reaches down and stands in front of me. Instructing me to place my small hands into the bucket, doing the same as he previously did.

Leaning close to my ear he whispers, *"Now turn and face the passengers."*

He raised the bucket above my head. Very slowly he follows

the same process William did to him. Slowly pouring cold salty brine over me. I shiver from the instant shock of the cold sea liquid as it slowly falls down my small slender frame.

Another soft whisper in my ear, *"Now turn and face me,"* he says as he slowly moves the bucket over one breast and then the other.

He leans in so only I can hear him say; *"You held the sick bairn close to your beautiful bosom. I want to make sure this deadly disease is removed from that area."* Continuing he says, *"Now rub the material of your smock together to make sure all of the child's puss can be removed."*

I do as I am told using my small fingers, I gather a handful of my garment and rub it together in a scrubbing motion. Not leaving my vision from his hypnotic Safire eyes. He pours more chilly water over my gathered garment. The cold seawater seeped thru my thin chemise onto my breast.

Leaning closer to my ear and whispers, *"I love how they got so aroused by the icy water. Ready for my suckling. Hoping dear lass, they will soon feel my tender lips."*

Planting a tender peck on my neck before straightening for the next person that stood in line behind me. I promptly move out of the way. Allowing the stream of doused sailors to move to the side of the ship to pull up the many lines that held the buckets. Pulling salty brine, onto the deck of the ship Hector.

The water bucket line worked handsomely, as each passenger and crew member was doused with cold salty seawater. Rumbles amongst the crew and passengers hoping this salty brine was going to help eradicate the deadly disease that has enveloped the ship, Hector.

The captain and the few able passengers were busy making the arrangements to move the infected passengers to a separate sleeping area in the hole of the vessel. Their bedding was brought on deck to be doused with buckets of salty sea brine mixed with Lye, the wet bed coverings, were then laid out on the deck to dry from the heat of the sun.

The Doctor worked efficiently diagnosing the many passengers and crew of more than two hundred bodies aboard the sailing vessel called Hector.

Everyone aboard the confines of this vessel prayed this saltwater wash will keep the infectious disease at bay.

Chapter 17

Later in the evening I gathered my dried personal garments, folded them, and placed them into my carpet bag. I turn to the bow of the ship, facing the horizon in the distance. My thoughts drifted wondering if we would ever arrive at this place called New Scotland. Or will we all die from this infectious disease that has swept over our vessels?

My chin resting on the rail I hum an olde child's verse my mom sang to me as a young bairn. I smell his presence before his large hands gently land on my shoulders, whispering the word to my humming tune.

"I saw a Man on the Moon, clouting Saint Peters shoon.
I saw a Hare chase a Hound, twenty miles above the ground,

I saw a Goose Ring a Hog, and a Snale to bite a Dog,
I saw a Mouse catch a Cat, and the Cheese that eats the Rat."

I turn to face him standing before me, he lowers and places a gentle smooch on my tender lips. Then turns me to face the distant sparkling blue waters and softly sings another olde Scottish Ballad, as he places his chin on my shoulder and softly whispers,

I love a Lassie, a bonnie Highland Lassie,
Could you see her you would fancy her as well,
I met her in July, popped the question today,
I'll soon have her all to myself, as me wee wife
Her father, cannot consent, feeling contented.
I hold her and seal my bargain with a kiss,
I stand weary, so weary when I think of my dearie,
You will always hear me singing, I have a lass that loves me.

She is as pure as a Field of Heather
A Bonnie we lassie I tell,
This bonnie purple Heather
I will marry my Scottish Bluebell.

I slowly turn to face his brilliant blue eyes. Unable to say a word, I raise my lips to his, placing a soft tender peck.

He pulls me into his embrace, his chin resting on my shoulder, and softly whispers, *"Will you marry me, sweet Maddie? I want you by my side forever. I am impassioned whenever I'm around you, my nights are sleepless because you haunt my dreams. Every breath I take hurts when I am not by your side."*

Placing his large masculine hands on my cheeks, he lowers and softly places a passionate kiss on my lips.

My legs turn to rubber. My arms draped around his waist for strength. Confident, if my back was not pressed against the bow of the ship. I was certain, I would collapse onto the deck boards. Mackie has woken these strange demanding desires my body craves. Always wanting more. My dreams are also haunted by his embraces and his enthusiastic kisses. How could I say no to his request? Wondering if this is what happens when adults fall in love.

Who would have the answers I seek? Whom could I ask? My mother would be the most appropriate person to advise me about love and marriage. But that is not possible and never would be possible. Confident I may never see her again.

I could ask Lady Fraser, but she is confined to quarters with that deadly Smallpox disease. Maybe, I should speak with Lord Fraser, after all, I'm in his care. Wondering, could I still be a childcare worker to his children if I was to marry Mackie.

What a dilemma I am confronted with. I have strong feelings for Mackie. Am I ready to accept his marriage request?

Oh! I am so confused Mackie has a way of turning my emotions and desires into wonderment.

He releases our embrace and leads me to sit on the deck of the ship leaning our back against the rail.

Holding me in his embrace he whispers, *"Maddie, I love you so much. No one else has ever stirred my heart the way you do when you are in my arms. Are you haunted by these same feelings?"*

Resting my head on his chest, I shake it in acceptance, confirming I suffer from the same emotional sensations he is talking about.

"I want you as my wife, I know it was a very strange way for me to request your hand in marriage. When I recited that song, my heart swelled so much I thought it was going to burst in my chest. The words came out before I realized what I was saying."

I slowly whisper; *"It was so beautiful; however, I need time to think. Will you be patient for my reply?"*

"O! Yes, my love, take all the time we are not going anywhere, we are confined to this vessel until we reach New Scotland."

"I know nothing about you, will you tell me where you hail from?" I inquire.

"I am a descendent of Thomas Lyon, 8th Earl of Strathmore and Kinghorne. He married Jean Nicholson."

"So, your royalty," I state.

"Not really, it was not the path I wish to go down I left that lifestyle to my older siblings. I was too adventurous. Wanting to travel and see what was beyond our homeland of Scotland. I joined Captain Spears on his last trip to the Carolines."

"How many siblings do you have?"

"Three older brothers, named George, Charles, and William, and a sister younger than me, her name is Annie."

"What are your plans when we reach New Scotland?"

He turns me placing his hands on my cheeks saying, *"To settle with my wife on a plot of land, farm it with tones of animal, raising a bundle of children."* He then gently places a tender peck on my lips. Continuing. *"Would you be happy to share this life with me?"*

I shake my head in approval.

He quickly pulls me onto his lap, devouring my lips with an enthusiastic succulent kiss.

A deep male voice brings us out of our passionate embrace, saying; *"I knew I'd find you both here."*

Releasing from Mackie's arms to find William blocking the sun with his bulky frame. He stood juggling three dinner plates in his hands. Handing them to Mackie, he quickly states, *"I couldn't carry our mugs of ale, I'll be right back."*

When he returned, he was not alone, a tall dark-haired girl

was approaching with a plate in one hand and a mug of ale in her other.

"I hope you don't mind if I invited Elsbeth to join us."

"Not at all," was my quick response, glad I was not the only female with these two strong strapping men.

"Hi, Elsbeth, I'm Mackie, this is Maddie, are you travelling alone?"

"No, I'm with my parents, Catherine and Roderick MacLeod, and my little brother, Thomas."

"Where was home for you?" I inquire.

"The village of Dundonnell at the mouth of the loch."

"What about you Maddie, where was home for you?"

"Down by Loch"

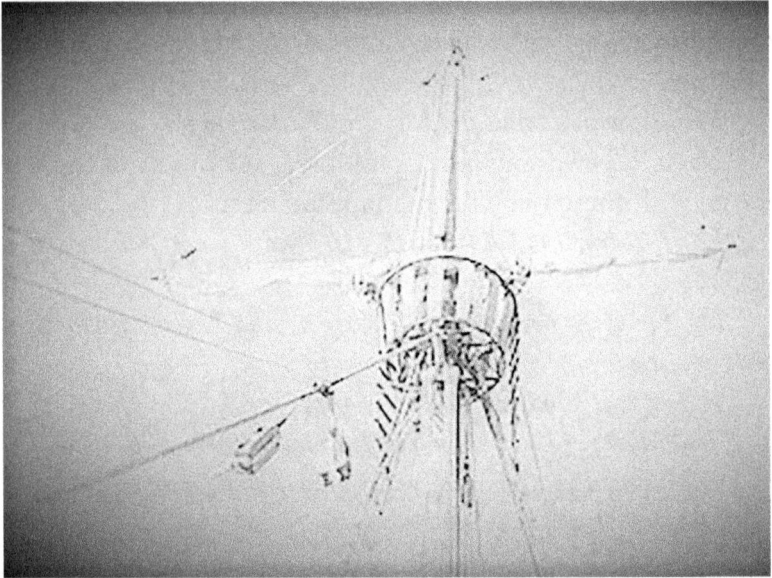

Chapter 18

A rush of commotions takes our attention to the stern portion of the ship. Mackie and William rise and rush to where several passengers were gathering.

Lord Donald Fraser reaches the deck boards and drops to his knees with his youngest child cradled in his arms, saying, *"My we babe has died, me precious we lad."* Mackie rushes to his side embracing the laird in his comforting arms. The lifeless child was held between the two large male figures.

I stood frozen in shock, unable to shed a tear. Overwhelmed at the site of two massive Scottish men in such a sad, endearing embrace. The small lifeless body of Samuel cradled between them.

William leaves my side, rushing off to notify the captain,

leaving the large crowd that gathered around this mournful site. The roar of the captain's voice, saying, *"Make way, make way!"*

William was on his heels, in his right hand holding a small square piece of sail cloth, in the other he held many lengths of rope.

He lowers placing a large hand on the backs of Mackie and the Lord, whispering soft words of comfort. William lays the sailcloth on the deck floor beside the two men. Lord Fraser gently places his small child onto the crisp white cloth. Then lowers placing a tender peck on his child's forehead whispering words, only Mackie and the Captain could hear.

The captain quickly wraps the wee bairn, sealing the wrappings with the rope strands.

Rising with the cradling child in his arms. William and Mackie had separated the crowd of passengers, creating an open walkway to the rail of the ship. The captain with Lord Fraser by his side walks slowly to the port side of the vessel.

Mackie pulls me from the crowd, and William does the same with Elsbeth. We follow in a solemn procession to the chest-high rail of the ship.

Mackie directs me to stand beside Lord Fraser placing his arm over my shoulder. William and Catherine moved to the other side of the rail beside the captain.

The captain speaks softly to Lord Fraser, then passes the wrapped child into his fathers' arms. He opens his black well-worn Bible in a loud bellowing voice he reads.

"Lord God,
by the power of your word.
You stilled the chaos of the primeval seas.
You made the raging waters of the flood subside.

You calmed the storm on the Sea of Galilee.
As we commit these earthly remains of this wee child,
<u>*Master Samuel Fraser*</u>
to the deep.
Grant him peace and tranquillity.
Until that day when Samuel, and
All who believe in you will be raised to glory.
of a new life promised in the waters of baptism.
We ask this through Christ our Lord. Amen."

Turning he places his hand on the broad back of Lord Fraser. Whispered, so no one could hear his words.

The small white-clad wrapping was released from the Lord's large hands and disappeared into the deep blue water below.

Tears welled up, slowly falling down my cheeks. My vision turns cloudy from the salty tears. Mackie pulls me tighter into his embrace as I say, *"I only had the wee lad in my care for a short time."*

"I know my love, he's in gods care now" continuing, *"Hush my love be thankful you had shared his love."*

The captain, places his arm over the Lord's shoulder, saying. *"Shall we go to my cabin for a comforting drink of ale?"* The Lord slowly nods revealing his acceptance.

The captain promptly turns to Mackie and William indicating we were to join him and the Lord in the Captain's quarters.

"What! He wants us to join him and Lord Fraser?" I inquire.

"Yes, he would like the four of us to join him and the Lord in a pint of ale for the Lord's son."

Having no knowledge of the burial ritual. I had never attended a burial service that was this personal and private. I had only been to two previous passing. The first I was a young child at the early age of six, when my grandmother, my maw's mother passed away. I was too young to recall what the grown-ups did after we laid my nan to rest.

The second was a church service for a classmate, I only attended the service at the church to sing in the choir with my schoolmates.

Entering the large living quarters of Captain Spier's cabin. I'm overwhelmed by its size. A large table was secured in the centre of the room with six wooden chairs placed around it. The back of the room had four large windows. My vision caught sight of the wake waters rippling from the keel, as the vessel swiftly moved eastwards.

The captain motions us to sit at the large trestle table that was anchored to the floor. He sat at the head of the table with his back to the large window view. Mackie and I took the two chairs to his right, and the piper and Elsbeth sat across the table from us.

Lord Fraser, chose to sit at the other end of the table, opposite the captain. As he sat, he promptly bent to place his elbows on his thighs, his large hands covering his face. Silent sobs could be heard through his cupped hands. The captain rose, approached the Lord, and places a large hand on his back saying. *"I am sorry for the loss of your wee bairn. I cannot say how you feel, for I never seeded a child of my own. However, I had many friends and crew that I partook in service to bury them at sea. It is a challenging task but must be done for all to allow their cherished memories to enter."*

A wooden platter of tasty fried bread covered in sticky honey was placed in the centre of the large table. Along with another tray that held, sliced cheese and morsels of smoked fish.

A deckhand was slowly moving around the table, filling the large mugs with ale, and placing the mugs in front of us.

"Come, Lord Fraser, you must eat, to care for your wife and remaining children. You are no good to them if you get too weak." The captain said as he slowly walked to his seat at the head of the table. Raising his mug of ale saying. *"Too wee baby, Fraser, may his passing provide us with a safe journey to New Scotland."* We all stood and clinked our mugs in support.

As I sat, my right hand slid over Lord Fraser's left hand that rested on the table saying. *"How are my Lady and your other children doing?"*

"My lady is gaining her strength; however, the children are not faring as well. Sarah is still hot with a fever and cannot keep food in her small belly."

The captain quickly signals the young crew member that stood by a serving table, to come towards our table. *"Go and inform the cook to make a large broth of soup for the ill passengers below."*

The Laird raises his mug of ale saying, *"Thank you, Captain, I'm sure a warm mug of broth would be welcoming."*

We sat for most of the afternoon, sharing stories of our journeys. Revealing tales of why each of us was aboard the ship Hector that was taking us to New Scotland.

Chapter 19

Lord Fraser was the first to leave the captain's quarters, advising he should go below and check on his wife and wee bairns.

The four of us also rose to leave the captain's quarters, thanking him for his invite and sharing his table of food and ale with us.

Shaking William's hand, he states, *"I was too quick to judge you prior to boarding my ship. Your resourcefulness and prompt action have revealed you are a tender-hearted man, always ready to step up under any happenstance."*

He then takes Mackie's hand and states; *"You are always one step ahead of every situation. Always prompt and ready to react when issues arise, I am proud to have you on my crew."*

The two of them respond with appreciation, as we left the captain's private quarters.

Mackie places his arm over my shoulder and brings me into his comforting embrace. William takes Elsbeth's small hand into his large mitt. We step out onto the deck of the ship to a full large moon on the horizon.

Reaching the rail at the bow of the sailing vessel Mackie points to the sky. He whispers in my ear, *"A falling star, quick, make a wish before it disappears."*

We watch cheek to cheek as it quickly fades into the evening sky.

He turns to place a tender peck on my neck and whispers, *"Did you make a wish?"*

His tender embrace and feather kisses have my emotions rising throughout my physique. All I can do was shake my head, indicating I had made my wish.

"What did you wish for?" he inquires as he turns me to face him.

I look up into his blue hypnotic eyes and speak. *"I can't tell you, for it may never come true if I was to reveal it."*

He lowers his lips, placing a slow seductive kiss, which has me weak in the knees. Releasing me he whispers, *"Mine came true."*

"But we just made our wishes, how did you get yours so fast." I inquire.

"Mine was to steal a kiss whenever I can."

"Come to think of it, I guess mine did as well," I say in a sheepish whisper.

"What did you wish for?" holding me in a tender embrace.

Raising my arms, stretching them around his neck pulling him into another amorous embrace. Releasing I say, *"To remain in your arms forever."*

86

"So, are you saying you'll be my wife, and marry me?"

I timidly shake my head in approval.

He raises me in his arms swinging me around, shouting manly howls.

William and Elsbeth come rushing over to where he had me dizzy from his swinging embrace.

"Is there a problem?" William inquires as he and Elsbeth arrived at our side.

Mackie quickly replies; *"She said yes!"* as he swings me around in another one of his embraces.

"Yes, to what?" Elsbeth inquires.

"To marry me!" Mackie quickly lowers me, placing a tender peck on my cheek.

William grabs Mackie from my arms, taking him into his arms for a manly embrace.

Elsbeth, turns to me saying, *"Congratulations, did he just ask you this evening?"*

"No, several days ago."

She turns to look at me in puzzlement.

Mackie pulls away from William saying, *"It makes no difference when. This evening is the most important day, because she agreed this evening under a full moon and a shooting star, making me such a lucky bloke."*

The four of us spent the warm evening embraced in each other's arms. Drifting in and out of sleep as Mackie cradled me in his broad grip. The four of us rose early, wanting to catch the sun rising from its watery bed. Standing at the bow of the ship, a streak of light beamed along the water line on the horizon before us. We stood frozen captivated by this magical event, as the golden globe was pulled from the deep blue waters into the eastern sky. Mystified by this beautiful, orchestrated performance. Wondering, was there a large hook pulling this golden globe from the distant waters? Rising ever so slowly spreading its sparkling shine across the vast crystal blue sheen. Enlarging, growing as it rose higher and higher. A breath-taking vision not witnessed by very many.

Chapter 20

As the days passed, this dreadful disease claimed more lives. The passengers' spirits were low as more wrapped souls were lowered into the deep ocean waters.

Lord Fraser lost Matthew the day after he gently released Samuel's small body to his watery grave. Two days later, his last child was taken from him and his wife. Sarah joined her two brothers at the bottom of the vast cold blue ocean.

Lady Fraser was allowed to remain on the deck after burying her last living child. The Doctor upgraded her condition. Her spots had dried and crusted over. Her body was scarred; however, all red pox marks were free of the pustules' contagious substance. She walked around the deck in the arms of her husband. Both hands rested on her protruding belly, praying that this child could stay protected in her swollen womb. Devastated that she lost all her children. Hoping this one would stay sheltered in her abdomen until they reach New Scotland.

Three out of every ten passengers died from this devastating disease called Smallpox. Disfiguring pockmarks caused by a progressive skin rash. Several surviving adults were left blind. Lady Fraser suffered diminished eyesight however she was cleared of mouth sores and red welts caused by this contagious illness.

No new cases arose, following the sea burial of Sarah, the Laird's oldest child. However, there was an increase in the deaths of those who had contracted this contagious disease. As each day passed, another soul would be wrapped in pieces of sailcloth and gently lowered over the side of the ship. Some days we stood and watch as three or more per day were sent to their watery grave.

Captain Spier grew weary as he recited those sad words over each wrapped deceased passenger. He no longer needed to read those troublesome words from his bible. The words were imprinted in his memory.

The number of deaths climbed; however, all were relieved there were no new cases. The last to die brought the total to eighteen (18) souls. Sadly, the majority were children. The crew was busy cleaning the hull of the ship where so many passengers spent their final days. Ridding the confined darkened area of any sign of the infectious disease. Beddings were stripped and brought up on deck to be washed and left to dry in the blowing sea air. The bunks were doused with seawater and lye.

The passengers were now permitted to come out from the hole of the ship and spend time in the sunshine. This reprieve only lasted for a brief time as the ship sailed closer to its new destination.

Chapter 21

It was late August when a sailor on the bow spotted the rough rocks off the shores of the Grand Banks. Word swept among passengers advising we should be in Pictou within the week. Ten days at the most. Mackie grabs me whispering, *"Not much longer and we should be in Pictou."*

We gathered along the bow of the ship as she sailed closer toward the shores of Newfoundland and Labrador.

Captain Spier recognizes the darkened bruised clouds on the horizon. He shouts instructions to the crew in an alarming tone.

Mackie promptly leaves my side saying, *"Quickly go below with Lord and Lady Fraser, for we are in for a great tumble."* He quickly joined his shipmates scampering up the ropes to the bellowing sails that were reefing to their limits, working with breakneck speed to gather the sails, and wrapping them securely. I followed the other passengers that were above deck as we were instructed to rush into the bowels of the ship.

The hatches were battened down, securing me along with Lord and Lady Fraser with the other Scottish travellers, Into the darkness with only a swinging oil lamp for light.

Our future was left in the hands of Captain Spiers and his knowledge of how to manoeuvre this vessel toward our destination. We had no choice, no place to go, no place to hide from the pending thunderstorm that was heading toward us. This brutal typhoon with its ferocious surges would be upon us in minutes. Expedience was required to seal and protect the vessel from the devastating attack these winds were going to hammer against our confined ship. The ferocious winds were tossing the vessel in a whirlwind of circles. We pleaded with him to turn the ship around and head back, hoping he would hear our cries and demands. We knew deep down this was not an option. We were assured the captain knew this storm was going to be extremely brutal and deadly and was prepared to fight through it.

I investigated the dimly lit cavern at the other passengers huddled in their bunks fearing for their lives. I cradled myself close to Lord Frasers' right side; his wife settled on his left. The three of us were being tossed around like toys on a child's floor. Wondering where on the vessel was Mackie and William. The last sight of them was on deck as the hatch was sealed and fastened. Recalling how they remained on deck, helping to secure the sails and loose items that were on the floor of the ship.

These concerned thoughts were soon lost in my screams, blended with the other passengers as we were suddenly tossed to the floor. Everyone gathered on the lower bunks. Anything higher was too dangerous. We could hear the howls of pain from the passengers who had received broken or damaged limbs caused by the tremendous tossing of our vessel.

Deafening cries from the passengers after hearing the loud creaking sounds from the ship's hull as each mammoth wave hit with brutal force. The three of us huddled together on the Frasers bunk. These winds tipped the vessel on its side sending us tossing onto each other's bodies as the Hector rocked back and forth and then to an upright position. Confined and frightened in the blackness of our quarters. It was not only the children's frightened sobs and screams but ours as well as each loud thunder and pounding of the large waves that kept hitting the vessel as it pitched in the rough waters.

With the passing of time, I wondered was this ship going to be my coffin if it sinks into the freezing waters below.

I worried if Mackie was safe above in the secured quarter.

Was there still a captain's quarter attached to the top side of the ship, I wondered?

The continuous creaking and roars of the vessel's structure as it tumbled in the churning waves and twisted howling winds. I crouched on the bottom bunk, mortified, and frightened as I leaned against Lord Fraser for comfort. His arms are locked securely around his weeping wife.

I began praying that the Lord Almighty would release us from this merciless punishment we were enduring.

Hours passed; how many I had no idea. The darkened confinements in the hull, made it feel like an eternity. Prayers were spoken in loud voices, not by whispers.

The calm of the storm settled the vessel to a bobbing movement. We sat relieved by its stillness only to be shocked by an uproar of another pounding wave, tossing us from our relaxed demeanour. Hour by hour, day by day we huddled, grabbing small portions of food as the storm-tossed us for days. We were completely unaware of how long we sat in the confined hull of the ship. It felt like an eternity. There were times I recited verses by Shakespeare from memory. Some of the men sang old Scottish songs. Rising to stretch our cramped bodies was difficult however necessary.

The calming movement of the ship brought us all to attention. I heard the soft voices of the passengers wondering was our ordeal truly over. We spoke in whispers, were we afraid to disturb the storm Gods? Frightened to accept that our treacherous ordeal was finally over.

Eventually, the calming blue waters arrived and calm the vessel for its journey. I found myself huddled in the depths of the ship, completely unaware that over a week had gone by before the tranquil blue waters finally came and prepared the vessel. Overwhelmed to hear the latch being released from the hatch doors above. The passengers nearer to its entrance gingerly moved towards the sunlit opening.

Injured and battered passengers slowly climbed the stairs that led to the deck of the ship. Rising into the blinding bright sunlight.

It was a struggle for Lord and Lady Fraser and me to rise from our cramped and aching positions. My small frame was covered in bruises that were beginning to form dark blue and black patches. A result of being thrown from our bunk multiple times. As we cuddled together on the Fraser bunk below deck, we persevered despite our bruised aching bodies.

Lord and Lady Fraser and I tried with great difficulty to stand, from our huddled battered confinements. We endured while cuddling together on the Fraser bunk below deck. Our bruised bodies were aching, from the constant pounding.

Along with our inability to stand nor walk throughout the tremendous tossing our bodies had lived through during our lengthy confinement.

I gingerly approached the opening to find Mackie and William waiting for us to reach the deck. The bright sunlight affected my vision as I slowly rise to the deck floor.

I am quickly grabbed by a pair of strong hands. His familiar scent assured me it was Mackie as I buried my face into his neck. Safely away from the glaring brightness that was hurting my eyes. His familiar voice was a tell-tale sign. I squinted to find William doing the same with Elsbeth in his broad arms her parent following close behind. Mackie guided me to the bow of the ship to our familiar spot we always gathered around. He slowly lowers me to sit against the bow of the vessel. Beside me sat Lord Fraser with his wife on his arm. The six of us remained for some time huddled in embracing comfort. Glad we all survived this horrendous ordeal.

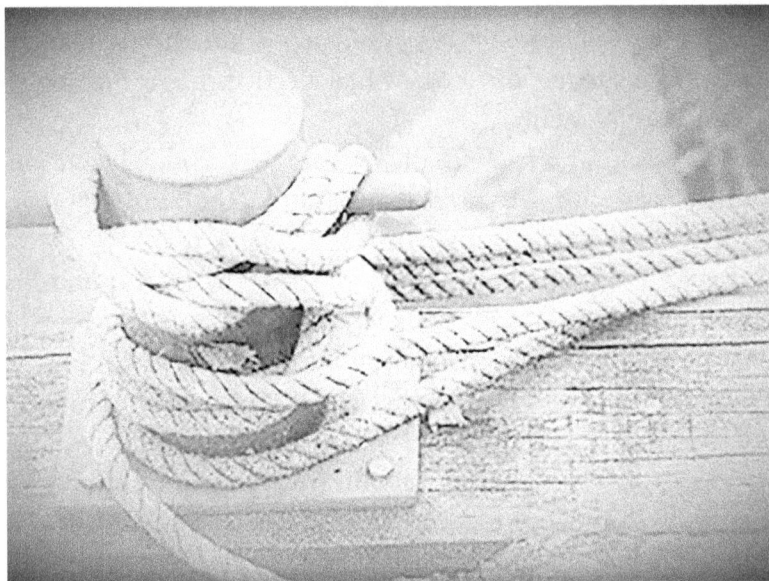

Chapter 22

Mackie's soft voice says, *"Keep your eyes closed until they get accustomed to the brightness of the sun."*

He pulls me into his broad arms, placing small kisses on the forehead of my face, saying; *"I am so glad you made it thru the storm unharmed. I worried so; my heart ached as each day passed."*

"How long were we below deck?" I inquire.

"Seven days, before the storm turned to move south. However, we lost the same number of days. The storm took us back to where we were six days ago. Our arrival at Pictou has now been delayed by at least fourteen days."

My vision is now accustomed to the brightness of the day I raise my head from his chest. Looking up into those beautiful sapphire eyes, Mackie lowers placing a peck on my lips, His tongue demanded entry. Accepting his invitation, I returned the kiss with a passionate response.

When we part, I whisper *"Your whiskers tickle."*

"I know, I also need to bathe."

"Me as well," I reply.

"William and I will gather the crew and we'll set up the divider like we did before so the passengers and crew can bathe." He leaves my embrace and disappears into the crowd of mingled crew and passengers.

Leaving the crowded deck and descending back into the bowels of the ship to retrieve a change of clothes and my toiletries. I also grab the bedding from my bunk as well as the bunched-up pile that sat on the Laird's sleeping quarters. Eyeing the bottom bunk where I found comfort during the long ferocious storm.

Reaching the bottom step just as a rush of passengers starts to descend to collect their items.

Heading for the bow of the ship, I find Mackie and William busy pulling up buckets of cold seawater. Several crew members were taking a filled bucket to the aft side of the vessel where the men would be bathing. The remainder of the crew was creating a curtain wall from the sails. It divided the men from the women and young children. Removing my garments down to my chemise with the embroidered top, I sit on the deck leaning against the rail. Undoing my plaits from my messy tangled hair, Mackie witnesses me struggling to untangle the bird's nest that has developed over those many days we were confined in the dark hole of the ship.

He walks over, I recognize that mischievous look in his wicked eyes. He sits behind me straddling a leg on each side of my backside. Scooting closer so our bodies were touching his front against my back. He lowers and places a tender kiss below my ear lobe whispering; *"let me do this for you."*

I slowly gave him a smile saying, *"Thanks."* His lips quickly come to mine for a tender peck. *"Now turn so I can untangle this mess."*

I do as I'm told resting my back against his broad bare chest and closing my eyes.

I am disturbed by a rustling movement to my right, I slowly turn to see what has caused this noise. I witness, Elsbeth sitting beside me and William lowering himself to sit in the same manner as Mackie's resting position.

I looked at Elsbeth's messy locks, realizing my head must look the same as her bird's nest that rested on her head.

Mackie has created a sweeping epidemic. More women with males sitting behind them. Going thru the same process. I caught sight of Lord Fraser doing the same to Isabella, his wife.

Mackie finishes and leans in placing another one of his tender kisses on my neck. I turn to say, *"Sit in front of me and I'll do yours."*

Looking at me in surprise, I promptly say; *"Look at William's head. Your mop is a bigger mess. So, move your buttocks here,"* I say as I point to the spot between my legs causing my chemise to gather higher up my thighs.

His sheepish grin with a sparkle in his eyes catches the movement of my garment exposing my legs by my parted thighs.

He sits between my legs, however, sitting too close to my groin. His left hand slowly creeps up toward my thigh. His finger tenderly slid over my bare flesh. I lean into his back my face buried against it. Enjoying however embarrassed at this seductive overture. I whisper in a raspy voice, not even sure it was me who was speaking; *"Please stop,"* taking a breath I continue, *"your too close for me to untangle your braid."*

He promptly turns his face inches from mine, saying; *"did you like that tender touch?"*

I nod, and then push my derrière further back for him to lean against my chest, to work on his messy black mop. Completing the task, I lean forward to find his eye closed, I whisper; *"Are you sleeping?"*

"No," he says turning to look into my inquiring vision. Continuing he says, *"I could stay leaning my head against your breast forever."* Then he quickly leans and places a passionate kiss on my lips.

Chapter 23

Before scrubbing my body with the cold brine, I add a wee bit of my rose water to the bucket. Removing my soiled chemise, I grab my washcloth and dip it into the cold bucket of salty seawater bathing my small frame. Dipping my head over and into the bucket I slowly wash my deep brown mass of curls. I reach for my old chemise and dab the excess moisture from my body. Placing my clean top on I proceed to wash my soiled garments spreading them on the ship's large floorboards on the deck. Lady Fraser comes to join me with the bedding. Saying; *"together we can manage to freshen these items and spread them on the deck of the ship to dry in the warm sunshine."*

"Would you like me to plait your hair," she inquires.

"I would love that, then I can do yours."

She nods her head in agreement.

We finish and notice several other ladies struggling with their young ones. The two of us head over to assist the mothers and help tend to their younger children.

"They don't like the cold salty water," one of the mothers says.

I reply, *"I'm not happy washing in cold salty water either, however, it is better than doing nothing."*

The group of mothers' nods in agreement.

A yell from the men's side of the ship, advising they could see land on the horizon. I turn and go to the bow of the vessel and sure enough, a dark streak could be seen in the distance.

A male voice from the other side of the private curtained area inquires if the white wall could now be removed. We check to see if all ladies have been washed and are freshly dressed. There were only a few younger children that still needed to be washed and dressed.

Lady Fraser, raises her voice to respond; *"Yes, there are only a few children that are in need of bathing."*

The mothers that has finished with their young ones took it upon themselves to help the other mothers who were struggling to wash their many children. The buckets were carried over to assist families in need.

The men released the curtain of white. They then turned towards the bow, coming over to gather the buckets of soapy dirty water and dumping them over the rails.

Everything was back to normal. The bathing was completed, and the white drape was put away. All the buckets were rinsed and placed back in their storage compartments.

Captain Spiers stood outside his quarters; a young crewmember was ringing a bell to gain our attention.

Mackie walked to my side placing his arm over my shoulder, together we strolled toward the stern of the ship.

Standing tall, the captain waits to obtain silence and have everyone's attention.

"We have just come through the worst storm I personally have experienced. Never have I ever passed thru a storm that covered, as many days as we had just endured. Ship Hector held fast against the torrents of rainfall and gale of blowing winds. She is a fine vessel." He then opened his black book to recite a small prayer.

"Why does God allow storms to come into our lives?
Does he use storms to wake us from our faithless lives?
Storms stir desperation in our hearts.
God's desire is not to destroy us amidst the raging storm.
But to strengthen our faith for survival.
Drawing us closer as friends, and families.
The Lord is our model of gentle dependence.
Storms can deepen our faith and trust.
We have prevailed and overcome this vicious storm.
Together, we will persevere and arrive at our destination."

Shouts rose from the passengers and crew as the captain walked down the steps to mingle among the passengers. Mackie and I weaved among the gathering of families. Expressing our joy that we had just come through the worst part of our journey. All confident that going forward no other setback would be as horrendous as these last several days we all had endured, survived, and together we travel through the most vicious storm that was ever thrown at any travellers.

All of us had gone thru this horrific hurricane and came out on the other side stronger and more confident that our destination is within our grasp.

Large mugs of ale and wine were passed amongst the adults to celebrate our survival. The warm soup broth was served in mugs for the children and those who chose not to partake in the spirits. The cook arrived with trays of food, smoked fish, jerky, cheese, and sweet Bannock, along with trays of various sweets.

Chapter 24

Mackie approached leading me away from the crowd that had gathered in the stern of the ship, taking me in his arms. Holding me, tightly he says, *"You smell like a fresh flower garden."*

"And you shaved your beard," I whisper, raising both my hands to feel his smooth clean-shaven facial features. I bring his face down to meet mine for a seductive kiss.

"Mmmmm, stealing a kiss. You have gotten bold dear maiden stealing a kiss from a man."

"You are forever stealing them from me. Why is it bold for me to want to kiss your smooth clean-shaven face?"

"Any time you wish to steal a kiss, I will never be disappointed by your demands." Lowering to place a seductive kiss, his arms

come under mine causing my own to reach over his shoulders and bring him towards me for an enthusiastic embrace.

Releasing from our amorous embrace, staying with our arms around each other. I witness many other couples doing the same. Embracing and kissing their freshly bathed partners.

Keeping me in his cuddle, he leads me to the bow of the sailing vessel, facing the faint strip of land on the horizon, his head resting on my shoulder. He whispers, *"There is going to be a lot of loving this evening. I believe Hector will be doing some rocking, and it will not be caused by rough waves, nor a pending storm that may arise in the night."*

Puzzled, I turn to face him saying; *"What are you saying? You have my thoughts confused."* Continuing I say, *"You say loving this evening, then you say rocking and not caused by the waves."*

"What I'm saying is many of these husbands and their wives will be doing more than sleeping this evening."

Embarrassed, I bury my head in his chest now aware of what he is speaking.

Placing his fingers under my chin, slowly raising my face. My vision downcast in embarrassed response.

"Look at me, sweet Maddie."

I raise my vision to focus on his crystal blue eyes.

He lowers saying, *"I patiently wait until I can make love to you and make this boat rock with our lovemaking. Soon I will have you in my arms and make sweet tender love to you. I will continue to wait patiently to make you, my wife. Do you understand?"*

All I can do is shake my head in approval.

"I need you to say you want to be my wife. Please tell me you will."

I rise to place a tender kiss on his lips and say, *"Yes, I wish to be your wife and have you as my husband."*

Pulling me into his massive embrace, *"I cannot wait either.*

My patience however is wearing thin. As a ship's mate, I cannot take you as my wife, it is impossible to marry and share my bed in the crew's quarters. We must be patient; however, I do want to marry you before we reach our destination. I am not sure if I can wait that long."

Responding I say, *"I have not spoken to Lord Fraser about your request for marriage. He is my guardian; I must have his approval."*

"You stay here, I'll go speak with Lord Fraser and ask for your hand." he lowers placing a tender peck on my moist lips and promptly leaves.

A short time later, Mackie arrives, with a broad smile on his face. Puzzled, by his demeanour, I lean my back against the rail of the vessel. He approaches placing his feet beside mine, leans in, devouring me in another one of his tender kisses that has my entire body rushed with emotional tingling sensations.

Releasing, he places his forehead against mine, saying; *"Lord Fraser has given me permission to have your hand in marriage."*

"What?... What about my position as a childcare worker?"

"They are no longer in need of a governess. At least not for many years, not until the baby Lady Fraser is carrying is of age."

"So, I am free to marry you?" I respond inquisitively.

"Yes, my Lady; Master Malcolm Donald Lyon is at your service." He states finishing with an elegant bow.

I stand bewildered, unable to take in the changes that have just occurred concerning my future. I boarded ship Hector as a childcare worker, and I may be departing from it as a bride. So much has happened in such a brief time. Why have these life-changing events regarding my future come about too quickly? We have yet to reach our destination, and my life has gone from being a daughter to a Governess as I boarded this ship and left it as a bride. This realization has just now set in as I slowly slide down and sit on the deck boards.

Mackie quickly kneels before me and brings me into his embrace. *"My love I did not mean to startle you with Lord Fraser's approval. You appear frightened. Are You?"*

I lean my back against the wall of the ship, saying; *"Everything is happening too fast. I boarded the ship as a daughter. Became a Governess upon meeting the children of Lord and Lady Fraser. And I may be departing as a bride on your arm. How could these events have happened so fast? I am so overwhelmed by these changes to my life, so much in such a short amount of time. My mind is telling me it is all a dream, and when I wake, I will be sitting in my parent's small home on the outskirts of Loch Broom."*

"No, my love it is, not a dream, it is all true. You do love me? That is correct is it not?"

" Yes, I do, but so many changes in such an abbreviated time. My mind is like a child's twirly toy spinning out of control. In such a brief time so much has happened to me."

I quickly rise, saying; *"I need time, please give me time"* as I run to the stairs that lead to the passenger compartment deck below.

Arriving at the tier of bunks, mine is at the very top. I climb and curl under the covers burying my head. Lady Fraser was laying in her bunk reading a book. She quickly rises and inquires, *"Maddie is everything all right?"*

"Yes," I reply in a soft voice.*"*

"Are you sure, I'm here if you wish to talk."

"No, I am fine I just need to rest. Thank you for your concern, my lady."

Chapter 25

Feeling a whole lot better after a short rest. As I stepped down from my high perch, Lady Fraser was sitting on her bed. She turned to say, *"Come sit by me, Maddie, you know, if you want someone to talk to, I would be glad to listen. Sometimes just talking to another person helps."* Continued; her hand patting the spot beside her, *"Come sit by me and tell me what worries you so."*

"Everything about my life is moving so fast."

"Explain," she says as I position myself beside her on the bottom bunk.

I begin repeating the concerns I expressed to Mackie before rushing below deck. *"So much has happened to me since leaving my family home, several weeks ago. I left my home as a daughter and older sister. When you and Lord Fraser arrived, I became a governess. I befriended Mackie, he has now asked for my hand in marriage. It is all so confusing."*

"*Sometimes things happen for a reason,*" was her reply.

"*What do you mean?*"

Taking my hands in hers she spoke in a confident and comforting voice, hard to believe she had this amount of strength after losing two children. "*Had the Lord and I not approached your parents about being a Governess for our children? Would we be sitting here together on this ship?*"

"*No, I guess, not.*"

"*Life sometimes is like a grand puzzle, all the pieces fit together. There are times we do not understand why. So, let us look at your life's puzzle that brings you to this dilemma you are so concerned about. We met with your parents, and you accepted our offer as a governess.*"

I shake my head in approval.

"*You arrive at the dock and meet up with Mackie Lyon and became friends.*"

Another nod of acceptance.

"*The Lord and I arrive at the wharf with our children, you immediately took over the responsibility as their governess. You were so good with them. They loved your stories and tales. The Lord and I were so thrilled you became part of our family.*"

Taking my hand in hers saying, "*You will always be part of our family, but not as a childcare worker. Our path in life has now changed, with the loss of my wee bairns.*" She pauses to dab a small tear that appeared in the corner of her eye with a small cloth.

Continuing she says, "*The Laird and I are no longer in need of a Governess, at least not until this bairn grows of age.*" She rubs her small hands over her protruding abdomen saying.

"*When you arrived at the wharf you met with a handsome*

young sailor by the name of Mackie and befriended him"

She turns my face to meet hers, saying, *"That was a good thing was it not?"*

I shake my head in approval.

"You fell in love with him and he with you.... am I correct?"

Again, I nod, as I fiddle with my handkerchief in my hands.

"Laird Fraser and I spoke often of your friendship with Mackie and how it blossomed so swiftly. Your love for each other is strong and enthusiastic. It is not much different than what Lord Fraser and I have. We had a very short courtship. We knew soon after meeting that our loving feeling meant we were to be together as life's partners. The Laird and I see the same love that is blossoming between you and Mackie. Do not delay, for love is too precious to let it linger with self-doubt. I see the same love in Mackie's eyes that I saw in Lord Fraser when we courted." Continuing; *"The Laird informed me Mackie approached him and asked for your hand in marriage. We both gave Mackie our approval. You are meant to be together; this voyage on Ship Hector has brought the two of you together in love."*

I turn to face her saying; *"Mackie said the same thing."*

"The same what?" she inquires.

"That this ship has brought us together as lovers."

"It certainly has, so how do you feel now that we had this little talk? What happens now?"

"You have eased my confusion. I do love Mackie, my heart aches when I am not in his arms. What do I do now?" I inquire.

"You marry that young lad, do not delay."

"I shake my head in approval." as she pulls me into a sisterly embrace.

"You will never regret your decision. Can I help dress you for your special day?"

I shake my head in agreement.

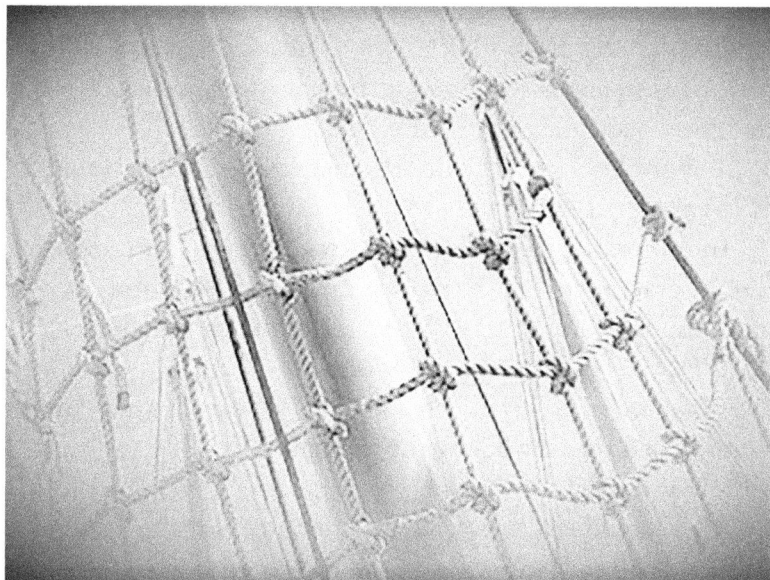

Chapter 26

On that early September day, the ship was bustling with excitement. We were approaching the ragged edges of the coastline of Newfoundland. sailing along the Grand Banks on the tip of Cape Race.

The ship's cook was busy rustling thru the sparse provisions trying to create a meal for the event that would be taking place in the late afternoon. The captain's quarters were provided with clean bedding. His personal items were gathered and taken to the shipmates' cabin next to the captain's suite.

Lady Fraser rooted thru her large crate of clothing. She was searching for a specific garment.

I stood alone in the captain's quarters with a warm bucket of water, slowly bathing myself as I stood looking out the large windows at the back of the ship. The warm water with the scent of rose petals felt good as I cleaned my small frame for the most special day of my life.

A slight knock on the door brings me out of my hazed fog. *"Who's there?"* I inquire.

The soft voice of Lady Fraser says, *"Tis me, can you open the door."* I grab my chemise to cover my naked body and open the door. Lady Fraser enters with an arm full of clothing.

"What do you have there?" I inquire.

"Your wedding dress," she says as she rushes toward the captain's bed that lay below the windows.

"Are you finished bathing?" she inquires.

All I could do was nod as I focused on the mound of garments she carried in her arms.

"Let's start with this," she says as she passes me a Victorian-style corset.

Sliding it over me she stands behind me tightening the laces, pulling it snugly below my bosom. It enhanced my waist to an hourglass shape. I next stepped into a hooped petticoat.

My Lady reaches for a deep rose-coloured satin dress.

I quickly say, *"No you cannot have me wear that exquisite garment. It is too beautiful."*

"Yes, I can, and today is your special day and I'm going to help to make it special and memorable."

I raise my arms allowing the dress to fall gently over me. My Lady quickly attends to the lace ties woven down the back of the garment. The long sleeves with a lace ruffle ended at my wrist. The low square neckline is trimmed with small strips of gathered lace.

The tight corsets below my breast were enhancing the size of my bosom, exposing a good portion of my naked breast. Bending my head to look down at my partially bare bosom alarmed that so much of my breast was exposed for all to see. I promptly turned to my Lady placing my arm over my bare bosom saying. *"You are going to cover this, right?*

"Absolutely not" was her reply, as she leads me over to an oval floor-length mirror that stood to the side.

I stood frozen looking at my image in the looking glass. *"Oh! My!"* I say bringing my hands to my face. *"This is me?"* I say alarmed at the vision of this elegant woman I saw in the mirror. Shocked that it was me looking at my own reflection in the glass.

"Yes, and you look beautiful, now let us do your hair." I sit on a chair that sat at the large trestle eating table.

Using white and deep red ribbons, she wove my curly locks away from my face, bunching them on the top of my head. Leaving several soft curls to fall along my cheek and down the nape of my neck. Then she took my black cap shoes with a large buckle and buffed them to a shine.

Standing in front of the large mirror I was shocked that it was me that was looking back. Lady Fraser came and stood behind me saying. *"You are going to make a beautiful bride, you look exquisite."* Leaning her chin on my shoulder, inquiring, *"Are you nervous or excited."*

"Both," I say my vision back to the mirror, astounded that it was me who was looking back. Surprised that my plain Scottish demeanour and appearance could be transformed into this pretty vision that smiled back at me.

A slight rap sounded on the captain's door; Lady Fraser went to see who it was. Returning she says, *"They are wondering if you are ready?"*

With a nervous demeanor I nod my approval.

She opens the door of the captain's cabin to allow me to exit first, stepping out into the bright sunshine. My first view was the gathering of over two hundred passengers and crew who stood on the deck and applauded my entrance. My focus turned to see Mackie standing next to the captain. He stood so dapper in a lengthy wine-coloured waistcoat. A white ruffled shirt could be partially visible under the high collar of the jacket. Knee britches with snow-white stockings. His jet-black long hair was elegantly styled into a braid that hung down his back.

On his right stood Captain Spears holding a bible and a collection of ribbons. To his left, Lord Fraser stood by his side. Lady Fraser places her hand on my elbow leading me towards the well-dressed men that stood just a few feet from me.

As I approach, Mackie takes my hands in his and brings them to his lips for a tender peck.

The captain stood before us holding a small bible in his hands and spoke.

"We are here this afternoon to join Madeline Ross and Malcolm Lyon in a marriage contract. Seeing that we do not have a church or a Minister, a Handfasting ceremony will be performed. These are two consenting adults who do not have family or relatives accompanying them. Laird and Lady Fraser will stand as their legal Guardians. This Groom and Bride have chosen today to bind their union of love. Marriage by means of Hand-fasting is a traditional symbol of binding hands, also known as the Bonds of Holy Matrimony."

We stood holding hands facing each other, my vision focused on his captivating eyes.

The Capitan takes the pieces of ribbon and wraps them around our wrists in a letter eight fashion weaving the ribbon around both our hands. He wove the ribbons from my right to Mackie's left hand until the cords were completely intertwined.

Opening his bible at the appropriate marked spot, in a loud voice he recites a familiar Hand-fasting matrimonial prayer.

"Arriving on this vessel, as two best friends. Your hearts now beat as one, full of youth and strength. Your hands work tirelessly together to build a future filled with love and happiness. These same hands will cradle and hold your children, wiping away tears from your eyes as your heart grow stronger with each passing day. As you age, your hands may wrinkle, but they will always reach for each other. Your hearts are forever bound by a love that will last a lifetime, joined in holy matrimony in the presence of beloved friends aboard the Ship Hector."

He then leans in and whispers; *"You can now release your bonds and embrace and kiss your life partner."*

Mackie releasing my hands twists the ribbons that slowly fell to the deck floor below. His broad outstretched arms reach for me, bringing me into his arms for a long-awaited tender affectionate caress.

Embracing, I surrender to his passionate kiss as I hear a roar from the large crowd that gathered around.

A familiar sound rises over the hushed crowd as William plays a slow tune on his pipes. Mackie leads me to the deck of the ship. Holding me tightly in his embrace we moved rhythmically around the large accessible area.

His lips close to my ear he whispers *"You are the most beautiful bride I have ever seen. My heart swells knowing you are now mine. I am the happiest man on this vessel this evening. Maddie, my wife, my life partner, and my best friend. Are you happy?"* in inquires.

I whisper; *"Yes, husband, I am happy to be your partner as we move closer to our new life in New Scotland."*

Our song ends, and I am quickly removed from Mackie's'

embrace by Lord Fraser. He twirls me around. I quickly see Lady Fraser in Mackie's large arms.

"I have the pleasure of dancing with a beautiful bride," he says as we spin around the deck.

"You and my Lady have been so kind and generous since I started this journey."

"It is you. I should be thanking you. How you cared for my children and wife during the lowest point of my life. I do not know how I can ever repay your compassion and commitment to my children. You brought joy to their short lives. These are the cherished memories I will carry until the day I die."

Our marriage celebration continued into the evening. Obtaining well wishes from the many passengers who had become so close during our perilous journey. Our celebration has lifted their spirits. This journey has brought us so close; we could have called them all family.

Chapter 27

On the western horizon, the sun was just starting to slide into the deep blue waters. We bid our goodnight to the party. Mackie takes my hand as we weave through the crowd of well-wishers, where he leads me toward the captain's quarter.

I quickly say; *"Where are we going?"*

"The captain has vacated his quarter for this night. It is his wedding gift to us." Saying as he looks at me with a sparkle in his eyes.

Reaching the door to the captain's quarters he picks me up and slowly opens the door. Kicking it closed as we enter. My eyes focused on a small lit lantern on the large trestle table. Beside the glowing amber, a tray of cheeses, along with several pieces of Bannock, and cured meat. Beside the tray two mugs, and a jug of wine.

He carries me to the captain's large bed; the setting sun was in full view from the windows above the bed.

Suddenly everything around me disappeared as Mackie places an enthusiastic kiss on my lips. Our arms entangle around our bodies.

Removing from our endearment peck, he rises to remove the wine dress jacket, placing it on the back of a chair. Slowly walking back to me he climbs on the bed, straddling his legs on each side of me. He has me sitting in front of him, his chest leans against my back his lips tenderly placing feather kisses below my ear. These tender butterfly sensations are sending erotic emotions throughout my petite frame.

He whispers, *"Do you know how beautiful you are? You took my breath away when you first walked out of the captain's quarters. I am not sure what I did, to have you fall in love with me. You are a rare flower that came into my life. How could I be so lucky."*

He has me in an emotionally erotic trance. Unaware he has released all the ties from the back of my gown. Arousing sensations awoke from the soft peck. His eyes slowly move over my bare-clad body, while whispering sweet words into my ear.

He raises my hips for me to stand. My beautiful dress falls to the floor. Slowly turning to look at him, I stand in the Victorian corset and white stockings. He slowly turns me to face him in these personally arousing undergarments. His vision rises, to meet mine. His deep blue eyes are glassy with arousal his lips slowly move over mine. A slow moan of approval rises from deep in his chest. He stands burying his face in the raised partially exposed bosom. He gently places tender kisses over sensual areas of my body. Deep moans came from deep in his chest.

Moaning with pleasure, he rises and places a feather kiss

on my lips and whispers, *"Turn, I'll undo the ties of your corset."* His hands work quickly, removing the lace constrants from the tightly fitting breast garment.

A rush of air fills my lungs as the feminine constraint falls from my slender frame onto the floor.

He remains standing behind me, his hands slowly moving around, placing them on my abdomen, gently pulling me into his large frame. I feel his hot breath as he places tantilizing kisses on my neck.

My body is reacting to these tender sensations he is showering over my small frame. Slow seductive moans radiate from deep in my chest, letting him know he has arroused my sexual desires.

His large palms slowly slide over my midriff gently, pulling me to lean into his broad chest. His head resting on my shoulder, her whispers, *"Do you know how much I love you?"*

All I could do was nod my head in aceptance. A soft moan rises deep inside my chest. His raspy breathing is causing my body to react to his large fingers as they slowly move over my exposed breasts. Leaning back savouring in his sensual touches, he moans in my ear. He has me in a drug induced trance of love.

I turn, saying *"It's my turn,"* I stand clad only in my chemise. Lowering, I remove his shoes and slowly lower his knee-high stockings. His last stocking is now removed; I slowly pull his white ruffled shirt over his chest.

He picks me up and places me on the edge of the large bed. Kneeling before me his eyes never leaving mine. He rises my chemise to my knees. Removing my shoes, he lowers my white stockings never moving his hypnotic eyes from mine. Our passionate love is being transferred to the other through our fixated eyes. He quickly pulls me into his embrace removing

Romance on the Hector

the bed covers from the captain's bed and gently lays me down.

Our tangled bodies roll over the thin mattress. His large hand manoeuvres my chemise gently raised over my head, I reach for the buttons on his britches, and he quickly slides them from his long legs. Our enthusiastic embrace, kisses over my body, then over his body. Our passion was devoured by each other's enthusiastic drive to please one another, loving each other, lips roaming to parts of the body I never thought would drive my passion beyond my control. So intense my body is demanding to go further, never wanting to stop, only wanting more.

Waking to a full moon shining through the window, it is a bright light on my face. Mackie's naked body was face down and spread eagle on the bed. His arm laying across my bare abdomen.

I gently raise his arm so I can slowly rise from the bed. I need to find the chamber pot and get something to eat. I softly move around the large room. I open a door and find a chamber closet. After relieving myself, I use the hanging washing cloth to refresh. Softly closing the door, I creep to the table and grab a small platter of food, along with a cup of wine. Ever so slowly I lower myself to sit at the foot of the bed. Watching the most perfect view of the moon hanging just above the water's edge. Mackie stirs, his arms sliding around the bed. I instantly sensed he was trying to find me without opening his eyes. Looking towards the window then turns his vision around the room.

"Maddie, where are you?"

"Here," I softly say as I sit at the foot of the bed.

He quickly turns, bringing me into his arms. The plate of food spread over the tousled bedding, and my mug of wine tips, grabbing it before it could spill too much of its contents over the covers.

Holding me tightly, he whispers; *"You gave me such a fright,*

I thought you left the room" burying his head into my chest.

He takes my hand placing it over his heart. *"Can you feel the pounding of my heart?"*

"Yes, why is your heart racing?"

"I thought you left me, and I lost you," he states with a raspy voice.

"Never my love, I married you until the day I die." Saying as I lower and cradled into his arms. *"Do you want something to eat?"*

"Yes, I'm famished and some of that wine if there's any left."

Rising he says, *"Where's the water closet?"*

I point as I rise to collect the tray of food and the jug of wine and bring them to the bed, I gather the damp wine soak covers placing them in a roll at the foot of the bed.

Mackie approaches with that wicked childish look in his eyes. He leans, placing a tender kiss over my left breast.. *"Do you know how much I love you?"* he inquires.

I shake my head, saying, *"Just as much as I love you. Now, come sit and eat."*

We devoured the plate of food along with a good portion of the wine.

He rises to take the empty containers to the table.

Returning he places his arms around me pulling me into his embrace saying. *"I could make love to you all day and all night if I didn't have to eat and put nourishment in my body."*

Gently placing me onto his lap. His lips devoured mine, taking me on another joyful journey of enthusiastic bliss.

Chapter 28

Waking, we rose early cuddling together on the captain's bed, shrouding our naked bodies with the sparse bed cover that lay crumbles over the large sleeping area. Mackie reached down to the floor where we had placed our tray of food and jug of wine the night before.

Finishing the remains of scraps of food from the tray, devouring these last morsels with the remainder of the wine.

My vision notices a grey strip across the calm waters on the horizon.

I pointed to it saying, *"What would that darken shadow in the distance be?"*

Mackie rises pulling his britches on, I grab my chemise that lay on the back of a chair. Alongside, the beautiful dress Lady Fraser loaned me for my wedding day.

"Maddie come look what I just found."

Rushing to his side, he pulls out a large roll of paper, unravelling the curled sleeve and spreading it over the large trestle table.

"It is a map of North America, created by Alexis Joillet, Look here. He crafted it in 1747."

I rush to grab our mugs and the empty jug placing the items on the corner of the roll of parchment paper. Ensuring the roll paper would remain flat as we examined it.

"We must be coming thru this area. This is the island called Newfoundland, and here on the left are the grand banks. The captain has manoeuvred the vessel up and around the Grand Banks."

"See here is the passage he is taking the vessel through. Pointing to the water area between the coast of Newfoundland to our right and this checked area of the Grand Banks. He will manoeuvre ship Hector down to the bottom of Baline Island. He will then turn the ship around the Cape de Raz and Cape Pine."

Watching as he moves his finger over the map, indicating how ship Hector would travel. He continued his pointed finger moving in a downward swoop then back up to move through a narrow passage between Cape Breton Island and the tip of St George Newfoundland. Passing around Cape Ray.

I inquire; *"why does he have to swoop so low thru here? Why can't he just sail straight through, reducing our sailing time?"*

"See these small dots, they signify a cluster of small islands. He must make a big swoop through this area for fear of hitting shallow waters and stranding the ship on a sand bar."

I point a finger to the narrow passage between Cape Breton and Cape Ray, saying. *"So, when he passes through this narrow passage where does he go from there."*

"He will turn the vessel south, passing along Cape Breton to our left and St John's Island on the right. Straight ahead where the map reads Island Verte. This little indentation is Pictou Bay."

A knock on the door brings us out of our inquisitive interest in the pathway Ship Hector would travel taking us toward our destination.

Mackie leaves my side, heading for the door. Opening, he greets the captain, advising him that he could enter.

Entering the cabin his vision scans the scattered disarray of rumpled bed covers. My wedding garments lay over the backs of several chairs along with some of Mackie's. The floor held several other discarded garments, along with shoes and stocking scattered here and there.

Standing beside Mackie, he pulls him into a manly embrace, whispering in his ear. Mackie shakes his head in approval. His face flushes with a twinkle in his eye as his vision turns to focus on mine.

"Good man." The captain said as he taps his broad hand on Mackie's back.

I proceed to gather my discarded items, aware that their brief discussion was all about our erotic emotional lovemaking throughout the evening, into the wee hours of the morning.

The captain approaches, saying, *"Just place your wedding garments on the chair and I will have a crew member take them to your sleeping quarters."* Reaching the table where we stood in front of the rolled-out map.

"I hope you don't mind, I was showing Maddie the map, explaining our journey around these treacherous waters."

"Not at all Mackie, you always were able to grasp the understanding of these nautical maps." He turned his attention to me inquiring; *"Did you understand the map and where we are headed?"*

"*Yes, and if I had any questions or concerns Mackie explained it very well.*" Continuing I say, "*I'll gather my garments and leave your quarters, thank you again for allowing us to share our wedding night here instead of on a bunk in the hull of the vessel. You provided us with beautiful service and accommodations, how can we ever repay you?*"

"*Call your firstborn after me,*" he replies with a laugh.

Mackie walks to place his arm over my shoulder saying. "*What if our first is a girl, we can't possibly call our wee lass, John.*"

"*No, but we could call her Joanna.*" I softly reply.

A large belly laugh comes from the captain as he reaches for Mackie's hand shaking it saying. "*Perfect I would love that, now I hope your first is a wee lass, Joanna Lyons is a beautiful name. I would be a proud captain if it comes about in nine months.*" Bringing Mackie into a manly embrace.

We gathered our wedding garments taking them below. Laird and Lady Fraser were sitting on their bunk as we approached with our wedding item in our arms.

"*My Lady I do not know how to thank you for allowing me to wear this beautiful dress and other garments for my wedding. You made our day incredibly special.*" I say, extending the armful of clothing toward her.

"*No, you keep them, I have many more carefully packed in crates below deck.*"

The Lord places an arm over Mackie's shoulder saying. "*I need not hear your request with the garment you carry that I provide for your wedding day. They as well are yours to keep. I have more packed in storage as well.*"

Mackie and I turn to look at each other in surprise. He quickly says; "*You are both so kind. How can we ever thank you for all you both have done to make our wedding day so beautiful and a memorable event.*"

"*No thanks are necessary. The bond of friendship we have developed during the arduous journey is the only thanks Lady Fraser and I require. When we arrive at our destination and step upon the shores of Pictou Harbour, I do hope we can establish our residences close to each other so our friendship can continue to flourish.*"

Lady Fraser holding her hand on her large protruding abdomen said. "*I would love it if our children could grow up together as friends.*" turned to reach for her husband's hand. She continues, saying "*hoping we can grow together in bonds of friendship, and continue this strong friendship the four of us have developed during this tragic journey. We should not part nor go in a different direction. Our relationship should grow and flourish stronger as neighbours.*"

"*I would love that my lady,*" I lean and bring her into a comforting embrace.

Laird and Mackie also embraced in a manly acceptance. Releasing Mackie, he turns his attention to both me and Mackie, saying; "*Moving forward in this special relationship of brotherhood, and sisterhood, we want you to call me Donald and my wife Isabella.*"

"*Oh, my! Are you sure? You have earned your titles and should be proud to pass them on to your children?*" I say in alarmed tone.

"*No, this is a new beginning for all of us and we no longer wish to carry these titles when our feet step upon the soil of this new land.*"

Chapter 29

Mackie and I place our new garments and apparel on an empty bunk. The four of us leave the confines of the belly of ship Hector, arriving on deck to the brilliance of the sunshine. Mackie places his left arm over my shoulder. It does not remain there for long. There were many passengers who had not expressed their wishes for our nuptials. They approach, pulling us into their embraces expressing their happy wishes for our handfasting union.

We hear the unique Scottish sound long before we reached his side. These haunting uncommon melodies drift over the ship. Floating over the white wake waters at the aft part of the vessel.

The sounds were disturbing the white seagulls that were levitating above us. In an open sky above soaring in a rhythmic dancing performance.

I notice William, his puffy cheek blowing in the reed of his bagpipes as he stood at the bow of the tall sailing vessel, Elsbeth stood at his side.

Approaching closer, I view her entranced puppy-eye demeanour. Focused only on the handsome piper as he played his bagpipes.

Arriving to stand beside her, she quickly comes out of her trance and pulls me into an embrace. Congratulating, both of us on our union of Handfasting.

Mackie eventually gets an opportunity to free himself from the many male crewmembers and passengers that were expressing their good wishes. Finally reaching my side, he lowers placing a tender peck on my lips, apologizing for his delay.

"Loving you from a distance overwhelms my heart. Happy that you are my wife, however, sad that you are not in my arms. My heart swells ten folds when you are in my arms." He says as he places another enthusiastic kiss on my lips.

My arms wrapped around his neck; I whisper in his ear. *"Were they all inquisitive about our lovemaking last evening?"*

"Yes, my dear wife, however, I left them all wondering with puzzlement as to what we did in the captain's quarters." I snuggle into his embrace as he turns me to view the coastlines of the green wooded foliage in the distance. Ship Hector meandered slowly through the cluster of small formations of land in the still waters.

Word travels about the ship, that if the weather holds and the winds stay strong, we may arrive at our destination in two days. Three at the very most. This news brought joyful excitement to the passengers and crew. They had been confined to the old wooden vessel for almost three months.

The sound of the pipers' bagpipes floats over us blending with the warm setting of the sun.

William and Elsbeth joined us at the bow of the ship with their meals, along with Donald Fraser and his wife, Isabella.

The Piper and Elsbeth looked at us quite startled when Mackie and I referred to Lord and Lady by their first names.

I certainly was having difficulty with these changes. Confident it would take me some time to call them by their Christian names instead of the titles they rightfully had earned as Laird and Lady.

Watching as Piper and Elsbeth were struggling as well with these new revelations the Lord and Lady decided to change as we approach closer to our destination.

Gathering at the bow, we discuss our renewed friendships, along with our hopes and wishes of continuing these bonds once we settle in these new lands of New Scotland.

We shared our decision about finding land close to each other when we set foot on the soil surrounding the community of Pictou. Revealing how we want to be neighbours and continue our strong bond. William and Elsbeth inquired if they as well could find land close to our settlement. Mackie and I along with Donald and Isabella agreed the six of us could create a small cluster that eventually would grow into a small Hamlet.

Mackie quickly rose, advising us he would be right back. He placed a small tender peck on my lips whispering, *"Don't miss me while I'm gone."*

"Where are you going?" I inquire.

"You'll see in time, be patient my Love." As he quickly disappeared towards the captain's quarters.

Returning with several rolled-up maps, he unfurled them out upon the deck boards. The sun was starting to set as the three men started looking thru the collection trying to find a specific one.

I sat wondering what they might be looking for. Captain Spier had done a great job getting us across the ocean to here and knew exactly where he was going. How could these three men know how to get to our destination?

Donald finally finds the exact map they were looking for. Spreading it out on the ship's floorboards we gathered around. I held one corner of the map Mackie sat to my right. The two of us were seated viewing the map from the bottom. To my left sat the piper and Elsbeth, on the opposite side sat Donald and Isabella. Donald was the one to spot the specific area these three men were looking for.

Pointing to the map, he says, *"We land here, at Brown's point, the west river runs down into this body of water, the bay of Pictou. A small group from the ship Betsy has settled here in Haliburton, along the west side of the river. It was brought to my attention that, this area further along towards Lyons Brook is of no interest to anyone."*

"What is that river called?" Mackie inquires.

"Some have called it North Brook others refer to it as Haliburton Brook. The captain tells me the fish in this area is plentiful as well as this" pointing to Lyons Brook. Continuing; *"Folks' tales say, the water is so thick with fish they jump from the cool river waters onto the shore."*

"This may be the best spot for the six of us to stake our claim to settle. If we reside here at least we would have fresh water and all the fish, we can catch. Until we get our dwellings built."

Continuing, *"Choosing this central location we would be close, to here."* As he points to Halliburton, *"and here,"* his large finger slides over the map that ends up at the community of Pictou. Moving his finger back over to Lyons Brook. *"I was informed there are a few Scottish settlers living here that arrived on the ship Betsy Six in 1767."*

Chapter 30

Arriving in Pictou Bay, landing at Brown's Point midmorning on Sept. 15th, 1773. Our limping vessel weathered severe storms. She slowly drifted into the mile-wide bay on the surge of the early morning high tide.

As Ship Hector slowly drifted into the bay of Pictou, we witnessed a rush of settlers that came to greet their new neighbours. These Scottish immigrants stood tall and proud wearing their Family tartan in a large colour display that stood lined along the shore. Among the settlers, I caught sight of several bare-chested tall men. Their braided hair had feathers sticking straight up. These dark-skinned men stood out among the pale complexion of the Scottish men and women.

Word travelled about the ship that these settlers had come

from Glasgow and Ireland on the tall sailing ship Betsy Six.

Captain Spiers manoeuvrers Ship Hector towards Brown's point, a trip that should have taken approximately two months to cross the ocean, had lengthened their voyage to just shy of three months. A trip devastated by the infection of smallpox, illness, death, and hunger.

The first vessel rowed out to meet the arriving new settlers. It took Hugh MacLeod and the body of his deceased wife. Piper William MacKay in his Scottish kilt stood at the bow of the small vessel playing Scottish melodies on his winded pipes, Elsbeth standing by his side in her family tartan plaids.

The passengers that were ill from the long trip were the next to be taken ashore.

I stood along the rail, and Mackie stood to my left, his arm over my shoulder. Isabella is at my right, Donald standing behind her in a loving embrace. We watched as the large collections of passengers were taken ashore with their small personal possessions. Watching the loving embraces, they received as they set foot on these new lands.

Word spread quickly that arrangements were made for a funeral service. That would be held later that day. A burial site had been created to bury the wife of Hugh Macleod

Donald, Isabella, Mackie, and I, were the last passengers to leave the battered weathered vessel that was home to us for almost three months.

Our small skiff was rowed onto a sand bar that ran from the shoreline into the bay. Mackie and Donald quickly jumped from the vessel helping to pull the rowboat further onto the bar.

I rose, however, before I could step out of the skiff, Mackie gently reaches for me, raising me into his broad arms. Mine rise to cradle them around the back of his neck. Carrying me up the bank onto the green turf. I notice Donald was doing the same with Isabella, barely seeing his face over her large protruding belly.

Before lowering me, he placed a tender peck on my cheek saying, *"This is the beginning of our new life together on this new land called Pictou of New Scotland."*

We were quickly greeted by the locals, who had arrived on the sailing ship Betsy. Landing in 1767 with one hundred and twenty settlers, after the landing only sixteen families remained in the Pictou area. So many had left, unable to farm the land due to the tall dense forest.

Setting foot on land after eleven weeks on a ship was unsettling. My legs felt like rubber. I was glad Mackie has his arm around me for support. We were able to remain upright however our stride was that of a drunken sailor. Weaving back and forth as we followed the earlier settlers to one of the three large log structures. We met with company agents Doctor Harris and Robert Patterson.

Patterson had surveyed the land for the Highlanders, creating lots, marking them as A, B, and C, on the west side of Scots Hill, west of Hardwood Hills, and west of Rogers Hill. Approx. 2 to 3 miles away from Pictou Bay. Travelling along the shore of Pictou Bay from the Haliburton River to the other side of Lyons Brook. The newcomers passed by several of these Log structures the same as the three in the community of Pictou. These homes were built and settled by the sixteen families that chose to remain in this area when they arrived on the ship Betsy Six.

Mackie, Donald, and William along with a group of male settlers travelled with a stocky bearded guide. Weaving thru the tall pines standing over two hundred feet in height, climbing over fallen trees, hatching their way through rough, thick brush. Having seen the first two options, the third they refused to venture towards. This was not what these three men understood nor expected, regarding the agreement prior to leaving their homeland of Scotland.

The deer forests back in Scotland had hardly any trees at all. What they did have were short and sparse limbs. The woods they had walked through were a giant forested homeland.

This was not what they had envisioned. Nor was it what they were promised by John Pagan's advertisement.

Donald and William inquired if they could pass by the area; they had reviewed on Captains Spiers's map. Reaching Lyons Brook, they followed the meandering bay coastline until they arrived at the community and river Haliburton Branch bordering Pictou Bay. The three men nodded to each other this was the area they wished to settle and build their homes. Agreeing they needed to research how to build one of these log structures using the felled large forest pine trees.

We were all devastated and shocked when advised that our years' free provisions would not materialize. As new Scottish settlers, we needed to build shelters before winter set in. This task was extremely difficult considering our limited resources. We had few provisions to last us through the reportedly harsh winters. Our only salvation was to rely on the families who had previously arrived on the Betsy Six.

The men returning to the settlement in Pictou were disappointed and frustrated, the land that they had just viewed, was not what they were promised. A large group of newly arrived settlers chose other options and places to settle.

Doctor Harris and Robert Patterson barred the door refusing them to enter.

Donald pulls out a copy of the advertisement that was

sent to the Scottish immigrants, stating what waited for them upon arrival.

> *"There's wood and there's water, there's wildfowl and tame,*
> *In the forest, good venison.' Good fish in the steams,*
> *Good grass for your cattle, good land for your plough.*
> *Good wheat to be raised and good barley to sow.*
> *No Landlords are there, the poor tenant to tease.*
> *No Lawyers to bully, no Bailiff to seize.*
> *But each honest fellow's a landlord, and dares,*
> *To spend on himself the whole fruit of his cares.*
> *They've no duties on candles, no taxes on malt,*
> *Nor do they, as we do, pay sauce for our salt.*
> *But all is as free as in those days of old,*
> *When poets assure us, the age was gold."*

The group of large Scotsmen frustrated and tired from their long voyage crowded like cattle in the hole of the ship Hector for eleven weeks. They stormed the building refusing to settle on the companies' allotted lands. They were also wanting to pick up food and provisions that were promised by these two men.

They were confronted with another shock, being told that they broke the contract, not accepting the allotted land from which they had just returned. Advising they would not receive any provisions.

Donald, William, and Mackie, backed by the other new Scottish settlers insisted the company honour their promise.

These two company agents continued to refuse their request. Doctor Harris and Robert Patterson stood strong with pistols in their hands, ready to stop the approaching new settlers.

The large group of Scotsmen overpowered the two men, disarming Mister Patterson, and Doctor Harris, and tying them both up.

The new settlers took what they felt they required to survive the dreadful pending winter. Leaving notes of what each had obtained and a promise of payment when they were able to settle their account.

Word of these atrocities eventually reached Halifax regarding the Highlanders' rebellion. Rumours quickly arrived saying the Archibald of Truro was preparing to march a militia and address this rebellion by these new Scottish settlers. These erroneous rumours were eventually squashed when Archibald refuse to take on this task. Saying *"I know Highlanders, and if these settlers were fairly treated, they would not have taken this action."*

Word of this drastic intersession by the Scottish highland settlers reached Halifax at the ear of Governor Lord William. He responded on behalf of the new immigrants to Nova Scotia. Orders were written by the Governor advising these new settlers had been promised these provisions by Robert Patterson and Doctor Harris. That no funds are going to be exchanged between both parties. What they had taken was theirs to take. No further action should be taken to retrieve funds from these new Scottish settlers.

A large group that had arrived on the ship Hector heard there were larger settlements further inland at the growing community called Truro. Choosing to travel the worn path of approximately forty miles toward this village, rather than stay and settle in the Pictou area.

Chapter 31

We, a group of six, heard rumours that a local schoolteacher might have a place for us to stay during the chilly winter months. James Davidson was kind enough to allow us to live in one of his log structures for the winter, along with other passengers from the Ship Hector who also chose to stay in the area. A total of twelve adults resided in the structure during the bitterly cold winter. We started planning to work together and build log shelters so that we could leave the teaching building in the spring.

Mackie, Donald, and William were fascinated by the strange log structures they found scattered along the shoreline of Pictou, Haliburton, and Lyons Brook. They were amazed that these massive trees could be cut and limbed to create such large and open dwellings with a central stone fireplace that could heat up the entire living space. The three men met with the owners of these unique structures to learn how they could create similar homes for themselves.

The men in the community worked together to teach Mackie, William, and Donald how to cut down these massive trees, strip the logs of their bark, and notch them to form tightly fitted corners. Each choosing adjoined designated lots. They worked together to build the same structures for each of their selected properties along the Pictou Harbour between Lyons Brook and Haliburton Branch. This tedious task kept them busy until the first snowfall. Securing the felled stripped logs, covering them with large pine branches to protect their efforts from the harsh winter elements.

Our first winter snowfall roared outside. The six of us sat on the floor together in front of the large central fireplace. Our men sat behind us, sitting between their legs, as we leaned against their broad chests.

We sat together, sharing stories of how our lives became intertwined. It was clear that the Ship Hector played a central role in bringing us together.

A sudden yelp from Isabella as she grabbed her large protruding belly. I quickly noticed the puddle of water that was forming on the floor between her legs.

Isabella turns her vision to Donald, saying, *"O! My, the baby is coming. I'm about to deliver our baby."* She gives another yelp as both hands cupped the bottom of her large belly.

Elsbeth quickly rushed to the pot that swung out from the fire pace, checking to see if we needed more water.

Isabella was ready to deliver her child. The three men stood stunned, frustrated what could they do?

Donald was the first to speak, *"What can I do"* he inquires.

Isabella was unable to respond as another wave of contractions was rushing over her large protruding belly.

I quickly turned to the three stunned males, saying *"Use the blankets and create a private area where Isabella can deliver her child, then bunch the bedding together to create a comfortable birthing area. Another should grab a few more buckets of water just in case."* Continuing I say, *"Grab as many pieces of cloth as you can find."*

The three shocked males scurried like trained soldiers. All set on their dedicated mission.

Elsbeth and I took turns sitting by Isabellas' side as she went into labour to deliver her child. Donald paced the creaky floorboards, on the other side of the makeshift curtain.

I was confident he was hoping for another son; however, sure his only concern was for a healthy child. Both he and Isabella were worried the disease from smallpox may have left the wee babe damaged.

In the early hours of a new day, wee Madeline Elsbeth Fraser was born. There were no signs of any issues with the disease that took their three other children. A healthy baby girl who was protected in her mother's belly through the trying journey we had travelled since leaving Loch Broom in July.

Word soon spread regarding Isabella and Donald's baby girl. Our new neighbours arrived with an abundance of baby supplies. They came with baby blankets and clothing. Along with a vast array of homemade baked goods and baskets filled with garden vegetables and preserves. A beautifully crafted bassinet inside was a collection of baby articles for the new arrival to New Scotland. Isabella was extremely grateful to accept these items for her newborn who comfortably slept in dreamland.

Our first Christmas in this new land would be arriving in the morning. A small fir tree sat in the corner with sparse decorations. A few items delivered by some of our new friends were placed under the tree wrapped in a cloth tied with a cord. Other neighbours arrived with homemade items and plates of baked goods.

Donald and William were able to catch a wild pheasant for tomorrow's meal. Christmas Eve, in this new land had us sharing stories of our adventure that took us to this distant place called New Scotland. We began recalling our journey aboard Ship Hector and how the old vessel brought us together grateful for so much. Wrapped gifts were not important. The friendship that has bonded us together is much stronger and the most important precious gift.

Mackie's arms were placed around my body hugging me to lean into his large frame. His calloused blistered hands rested over my belly, he leans close to my right ear and whispered. *"You seem to have put some weight on since we wed, you no longer have a flat tummy."* He slides his large palms over the small bump in my belly. *"Have you been sneaking treats from the sweet cupboard, where we stashed those Christmas baked goods provided by our new neighbours?"* He teasingly inquires.

I was hoping to have a little more time before revealing my news. The beginning of a new year would reveal my pending condition. It would confirm that my third monthly curse has passed. Hoping to have a few more days before informing him what I thought these changes to my petite frame meant. The first of the year would confirm what Isabella and I were excited about.

Would a few more days really make any difference? I wondered.

If Mackie notice the changes to my body, then that confirmed our suspicions.

I slightly turn leaning my head on his left shoulder, placing my hand over his as they rested over my small protruding abdomen. and whisper. *"My Christmas gift to you is here,"* as I slide his hand over my entire abdominal belly.

He quickly shifts our posture so that he is looking directly into my vision. His eyes gleamed like crystal with excitement.

"Are you saying that you carry my child? Is that the gift you are speaking of?"

I shake my head in approval.

He quickly pulls me into his embrace locking his lips on mine in a passionate kiss.

Quickly rising bringing me to stand with him, he pulls me into a comforting embrace, twirling me around the open floor.

Donald was the first to react to our circular twirl of excitement saying, *"What has the two of you so excited?"*

My vision on Isabella, she gives a slight nod, and I do the same confirming our secret.

Mackie excitedly says, *"Maddie has given me the best Christmas gift a man could ever wish for."*

Donald quickly reacted saying. *"And what would that be? None of us had the time to make or create any kind of Christmas gift."*

"She carries my child" he shouts with excitement.

Everyone quickly stood to take Mackie and me into a group hug. The six of us jumped around in excitement and congratulations.

I lay curled in Mackie's broad embrace, hearing his rhythmic nasal sound assuring me he is was in a deep sleep. Not me; I lay restless, unable to let the night slumber invade my petite frame. My vision focused on the small Christmas tree that sat in the corner. So sparse and frail, however beautiful with its few homemade decorations. A few pinecones and a paper chain connected by loops. One linked to the next. Weaving gently over the green brittle foliage.

Watching the flickering glow from the fireplace, dancing over the chain-coloured links. Reflecting on my journey since leaving my family home early last fall.

My life also has many links that have brought me here on this warm Christmas Eve. Curled in the arms of a man I love, taking comfort in his embrace.

It all began with a series of interconnected events that brought us together, much like a paper chain that I see hanging on our Christmas tree. Each link is attached to another, forming a seamless bond.

The chain started when Donald and Isabella, approached my family on that brisk September day. Requesting I join them as a governess to care for their children. Had it not been for that incident, I would not be here today.

Reflecting on this, I realize that I played a crucial role in bringing this paper chain together, and without my involvement, the others may not have been here either. I look around at my new family, sleeping soundly. Over to the side were Donald and Isabella. Recalling when I accepted their offer of being Governess for their children. These three connected links were created with my acceptance.

On a brisk summer day, arriving at the dock in Loch Broom. That sun-baked morn, I encountered William the Piper. Another link became attached to my chain of life.

My vision then captured a handsome deckhand called Mackie as he approached offering me his shirt to wipe away my concerned tears. This encounter is what bonded all the others to my chain of life. The last link circling our family chain was the piper falling in love with Elsbeth, and now a dear friend to us all. Having this precious bond with one another was our most valuable gift, no warped presents were required.

This bond of friendship is linked together, new beginnings, all because of our sea voyage, which brought us to this new community called Pictou, New Scotland. Aboard the tall sailing ship, *"Hector."*

Author Biography

Marianne Guimond White, is a resident of Nova Scotia, a mother of two grown children. Her passion for writing quirky little phrases, and short stories, began when she was a young teenager. Responding to a contest in a local newspaper requesting submisions for the first two lines of a song. She was ecstatic when the results arrived by mail informing her that her short stance was their third choice.

Another interesting published short story titled; *"Three Rings,"* a tale about a new bride who accidentlly brought the Toronto Transit Subway System to a halt during an early morning commute.

Her funny tale called *"Brothers and Sisters"* appeared in an Anthology. A comical story how a family of ten children, eight females and two boys. Residing in a home with only one bathroom. How the brothers' silly antics caused them to steal quality time from their siblings.

A widow who lovingly celebrated over fifty years of marriage. Her creative poetry and short stories were many as she traveled with her husband in their motor home to beautiful destinations within Canada.

This historical romance is her first published novel.

CPSIA information can be obtained
at www.ICGtesting.com
Printed in the USA
JSHW011949230723
45113JS00005B/20

9 781739 042608